PHASE 6

PAUL TEAGUE

The Secret Bunker Trilogy

Book 1 - Darkness Falls

Books 2 - The Four Quadrants

Books 3 - Regeneration

The Grid Trilogy

Book 1 - Fall of Justice

Book 2 - Quest for Vengeance

Book 3 - Catharsis

With Jon Evans

Book 1 - Incursion

Book 2 - Armada

Book 3 - Devastation

WORLD HEALTH ORGANIZATION GUIDANCE

Phase 6, the pandemic phase, is characterized by community level outbreaks in at least one other country in a different WHO region in addition to the criteria defined in Phase 5. Designation of this phase will indicate that a global pandemic is under way.

PROLOGUE

Senator Rose Kingston was feeling smug. She'd seen off Bryce Kincade for the third time that month. Every time he tried to nibble a bit more away from the newly formed state constitution, she'd slap him down. The world might be heading for hell in a handcart, but some of them still took a pride in their civic duty. And she'd protect the interests of the city until her dying breath.

She poured herself a glass of brandy, luxuriating in the taste. Brandy was becoming as hard to find as a decent cup of coffee. She had her own stash of that in the cellar too. There was no point in being a City Senator if it didn't bring with it a few favours.

And she'd jumped the queue for the new VaXX programme. At least she could thank Kincade for that. He'd prioritized all senior government members, bringing in Dr Julius Labatt, no less, to oversee the process. They even avoided the needles – this latest shot was administered using a revolutionary new technique. At least, that's how it was for the privileged, the needles would remain for some time for the remainder of the population.

The public would have to wait some time before they got this vaccine. Potentially, it could stop another mutation. That would buy everybody some much-needed time.

Rose finished off her brandy and walked up the long, imposing oak staircase to her bedroom on the first floor. There had been talk of Fortrillium requisitioning property across the city. *Nonsense!* she'd declared, fearful of losing her sumptuous home, which was paid for out of the public purse.

She pulled back her sheets and made herself comfortable in the bed, the empty pillow beside her a constant reminder. She missed Edward, her grief still raw and intense. Knocked down in the road by a hit-and-run driver, his death had been a terrible shock. There were no witnesses, but he hadn't suffered, she'd been assured, it would have been over in a matter of seconds.

Rose drifted off to sleep, thinking about her husband, remembering when they were young and their whole lives had been ahead of them.

In the morning Senator Rose Kingston's bed was empty, although there were signs that it had been slept in. The room had been locked from the inside and the house had remained secure until the housekeeper entered at nine o'clock.

When the alarm was raised and the investigations began, there was no indication of foul play. CCTV footage taken from inside the residence showed that nobody had entered or exited the building and Rose had never left the bedroom. When records were checked, there was no evidence that Senator Rose Kingston had ever existed. It was as if she'd been wiped off the face of the planet, as if she'd been completely deleted.

It was not the first time this had happened. Only the

week before, Senator Mel Hargreaves had disappeared, once again without a trace. At first it was assumed that there must be some administrative error – he couldn't have vanished into thin air. Hargreaves had spoken out vociferously against further fortification of the state borders, but he'd been shouted down by supporters of Bryce Kincade. In fact, Bryce Kincade was the only person involved in governing Sector 4 who didn't seem to be at all concerned by the mysterious disappearance of the much-respected senators.

CHAPTER ONE

Laney Price could feel the cool metal of Richter's gun pressing against her temple. This wasn't how she'd planned on the day working out.

The children had woken up too early, that wasn't the best start. Laney had gone to bed with a raging temperature, her head pounding. Within an hour of turning out the light, her sheets were sodden with sweat. She fell asleep praying that the children wouldn't catch her flu, but she'd known it was too late as she woke to their coughing before the weak morning light had filtered through the frayed cotton blind.

She knew the drill. If the neighbours heard the sounds of illness from the apartment next door, it would raise the alarm. It was easy enough to hide it in herself. In a warm scarf and a winter hat she could pass as tired or run down. But the children were too young to understand how important it was not to make a fuss. Their noses were streaming, their throats sore, and they wanted to let the whole world know about it. But the minute they did, the full force of Fortrillium would come down on them.

It was difficult enough being a lone parent. She'd had to

manage on her own since Evan had been called away to the checkpoints. Sure, the money came in as regular as clockwork, but with the food shortages beginning to bite, it wasn't much use. If she could only get her hands on some medicines – paracetamol or aspirin – anything to get her temperature down. And something to quieten the kids too.

She turned the volume up on the flat screen. There seemed to be fewer and fewer entertainment programmes these days. It was almost wall-to-wall news, hardly suitable viewing for the kids.

Bobby sat in his chair, crying, coughing and spluttering. He was three years old and had every intention of making Laney's life as difficult as possible. Every time she urged him to be quiet, plying him with toys or cereal treats, he did the opposite, ratcheting up the volume. It was as if he wanted the neighbours to know how she'd defied the government.

Meanwhile, Nina was placid – too placid, her face scarlet with the terrible heat which was ripping through her body. Laney placed a cool cloth against the child's forehead, urging the fever to break, willing them all to get better.

She could barely remember what it was like to pop into the doctor's surgery or make a casual call to the pharmacist. It was some years since she had made the decision to keep off the radar. Evan had warned her that she was putting them all at risk, but Laney knew it was the only way she'd be able to get her family away from Sector 4. They had to be ready when the time came.

Bobby began to whine again and Laney edged up the volume of the flat screen. There was a knock at the door. She cursed under her breath, it was only just past six o' clock and already she'd got the attention of the neighbours.

She placed a handful of cereal pieces on the tray of

Bobby's chair, made sure that Nina was safely on her back on the blanket, and then closed the living room door. As she made her way to the front of the apartment, she glanced in the mirror in the hallway. Her hair was damp with sweat, her face grey with exhaustion, and she was still in her dressing gown. She looked as ill as she felt. There was no hiding it from whoever was knocking.

She opened the door, terrified it might be them.

'Mrs Sellick, how good to see you. Is everything alright?'

She began to breathe again.

Mrs Sellick was floor twenty-seven's resident busybody. Nothing escaped the woman. She had a sixth sense for things that weren't right. And her antennae were twitching now. Aged eighty-five, some years previously she'd been the happy recipient of two new knee joints, courtesy of the state. She was also one of Sector 4's first pancreatic cancer survivors, a miracle at the time. Unfortunately, she showed her gratitude for her excellent health by becoming a zealot for the creeping changes that were emanating from Fortrillium on a near-daily basis. And that meant an early morning knock for Laney.

'Good morning, Laney. Are the children alright? I thought I heard coughing. You look terrible. Is everything okay?'

The woman could smell a rat. Laney thought she'd suspected for some time. She was always asking if the kids had received their latest VaXX. She'd fuss about them, looking for any sign.

'Oh, we're fine, Mrs Sellick. Thank you for checking. Was the sound of the flat screen disturbing you? I know it's early. I'll turn it down a little. I was trying to listen to a feature on the News Feed and the kids were being a bit rowdy. You know how it is.'

'My dear, you're sweating. You look quite ill.'

She let the words hang there, waiting for Laney to respond.

'It's been difficult with Evan away. I'm sure you understand. The heating's playing up, it's running far too hot. I feel like I'm about to pass out. It must be bad if you've noticed it.'

Laney attempted to laugh, but it was lame and Mrs Sellick knew it. Right on cue, the sound on the flat screen quietened and Bobby coughed.

'You'd better go back in there and make sure he's not choking on his breakfast. You know what toddlers can be like with their food. Would you like me to come in and help, my dear?'

She'd smelled blood and wanted to feast on some red meat. Laney wouldn't give her the satisfaction. Bobby's coughing subsided. Laney tried her best not to show the relief on her face.

'Sounds like he's okay now,' said Mrs Sellick, her eyes narrowing. 'How is Evan getting on at the checkpoints? He's doing fine work out there. We need more patriots like him. If it wasn't for those young men, the food shortages would be worse. Not a day goes by without me wanting to thank them.'

'He's fine, Mrs Sellick. It can be difficult, you know, what with the kids. But as you say, he's protecting the state line and keeping us safe. It's important work. The world is crumbling around us. Who even thought that it would come to this?'

Bobby coughed again, and then began to cry. Nina followed. The wailing was persistent. These were not whining children, they were clearly in some discomfort and Sellick knew it. Would her feelings of gratitude for Evan's work encourage her to keep her mouth shut? Or would she share her concerns with the Troopers, and that would be the end of it?

As she closed the door, Laney watched Mrs Sellick glide across the landing to her own apartment. Not that many years ago women like her would have cursed their luck being so many floors up on the high-rises, but Mrs Sellick looked barely fifty. The medical advances had been truly amazing.

Laney had a suitcase packed under the double bed. She didn't know where she'd run to, but she'd made an agreement with Evan before he left on his latest tour of duty. *If we become separated, search for me among the NVs, that's where I'll be. If they really exist, that's where you'll find me.*

But how could she think of running with a one - and three-year-old? To go anywhere, she had to take the double buggy. Just using the lift was a struggle. And how would she find the NoVaXX – if they even existed? She turned the volume down on the flat screen, not wanting to encourage further interference from her suspicious neighbour.

A news item caught her attention. There had been more overnight clashes on the state border, more breaches from Sector 29. They had it hard over there, but it was every state for itself now. Experts were referring to it constantly as Phase 6. Dissolution had begun. She worried about Evan again. That was not his posting, but sometimes they moved the troops about, depending on where the trouble flared up. It was possible he'd been involved in the violence.

Nina was lying silently again, too quietly for a one-year-old. She stared blankly into the air, her breathing labored, the little hair she had dripping with sweat. Was it true what she'd heard? Could she get medicine out there on the streets of the city without attracting the wrong sort of attention? As

Laney sat by her daughter, dabbing her brow with the moistened cloth, she wondered if she'd been foolish to rely on her instincts. Perhaps she should have followed the crowd.

There was another knock at the door, heavier this time. Curse that Mrs Sellick. She'd turned down the volume. What was she fussing about now?

'Look after your sister, Bobby!' she urged, as if it would make any difference to the three-year-old.

She didn't even bother closing the inner door. She was minded to tear into Mrs Sellick for disturbing her again. But when she opened the door, it wasn't Mrs Sellick in front of her.

'Laney Chase, ref: VB23. I'm entering these premises under section 9 of the NoVaXX State Directive. We suspect that you have at least two persons in this apartment who have not received their latest shots. Dr Baker, please go ahead.'

For a second, Laney considered resisting, maybe even attempting to close the door on them. She'd seen this man before. His name was Richter. He seemed to show up wherever there was trouble.

A crowd was gathering in the corridor. They'd been woken by the sounds of heavy boots and knocking. These were her neighbours. Now they were looking at her as if she was some stranger they barely knew.

The doctor breezed into the hallway and made directly for the children. Laney ran after him. He held out an electronic device, out of which came a needle. All those medical advances and still they used needles. Without a word of warning or reassurance, he took a blood sample from each of the children. Bobby protested loudly, Nina just lay there.

She'd been wrong, she knew that now. Her stupid

idealism and crazy notions about getting away from the city. Her ridiculous conspiracy theories. Now she'd put them all in danger, including Evan.

The doctor checked the instrument. He nodded to Richter, who spoke into a Comms device concealed within his heavy black breastplate. In one swift movement, Richter drew a weapon from its holster and placed it to her head. The metal felt cool and soothing against her burning forehead, it was almost a relief.

'Laney Chase, ref: VB23, Apartment Block 19, Floor 27 – you are charged with malicious intent against the state. Child 1 will be terminated. Child 2 will be taken into state care—'

'No! No! You can't do that. She's only a baby, for God's sake ...'

Dr Baker drew a second device from his pocket and pressed it against Nina's neck. She didn't flinch as she continued to stare up towards the ceiling, then her eyes closed gently. Laney began to scream as two men dressed in yellow HazMat suits walked into the room and cocooned the tiny body in black webbing. Laney dropped to the floor, shrieking at the doctor, pleading now for Bobby's life.

A third man in a HazMat suit roughly unbuckled the child from his chair and placed him into a plastic incubation unit, ignoring his cries. Laney screamed and shouted, but Richter held her steady, his clasp on her arm firm and secure. Not once did the barrel of his weapon move from her forehead.

He hauled her to her feet and led her out towards the corridor where a sizable crowd had gathered.

'Feckless NoVaXX!' somebody shouted from the back.

'Where is she?' Laney muttered, searching through her tears for the woman who'd done this to them, Mrs Sellick the snitch. She was nowhere to be seen. Richter pulled her up abruptly in front of the residents.

'Sector 4 would like to remind you that the VaXX programme is compulsory and that failure to attend for the latest shots will result in punitive measures. Fortrillium and the future of our population relies on your full compliance.'

He pressed a small device directly into the side of Laney's neck. The last thing she saw before dropping to the ground was her husband, Evan, standing beside Dr Baker and chatting casually, as if nothing had happened.

***

'It always impresses me when I see you do that!'

Alex Brady walked out from behind the tree which had been concealing him from view. He realized that Carlos would have known he was there all along, but he didn't want to disturb him. He loved to see his friend handle the sword so expertly.

'Hey, Alex, good to see you! Is it that time already? I got carried away.'

Carlos placed the katana into its sheath. Alex wanted to be nowhere near that blade. He'd just watched Carlos slice through three cabbages, one after the other, after throwing them into the air with his spare hand. They were now lying on the floor, perfectly cut through the centre.

'Do you want one?' Carlos asked, ready to throw one of the half cabbages towards his friend. 'There's not much point being the son of a cabbage farmer if I can't share them among my friends!'

Alex smiled and held out his hands to catch it.

'My mum will be grateful for this, thank you. I'm sick to death of eating cabbage, but I guess beggars can't be choosers. If we grow cabbage, we should eat cabbage. I'd kill for some carrots though!'

'Sorry, no can do, my friend! Cabbage it is, until the State commandeers our land. It can't be much longer now.'

'You really think it's going to happen?'

'Let's put it this way, I've started carrying this!'

Carlos pulled out a wakizashi sword, which he had concealed inside his loose-fitting trousers.

'My God, Carlos. What do you intend doing with that?'

'Nothing, yet. But you can never be too sure. This thing with Fortrillium ... it's getting serious. They seem to have more power than the President.'

'I still think it'll work itself out.'

That's what Alex had been telling himself since Audra disappeared. It was almost one year to the day. No word, no letter and no trace. She'd just vanished.

Sensing his friend returning to that dark place, Carlos changed the subject. Alex had been running steady for some weeks now, but he'd been like a man obsessed when Audra first went missing.

'She's the love of my life,' he'd say. 'I may only be nineteen, but she's the one. We'll die together, me and Audra. We were meant to be.'

At an age when most kids were still finding out who they were, Alex had a wonderful certainty about his girlfriend. It had hit him hard when she disappeared.

'Let me put the katana back in the house and I'll be with you. Mustn't miss the latest programme. You know what happens to a NoVaXX.'

Carlos Matiz was wealthy beyond Alex's imagination. At least, his dad was. They owned a huge house close to City Park, all paid for from cabbage sales. Carlos took no interest in the business and seemed embarrassed by the wealth – he was more comfortable chatting to his friends in their high-rise apartment blocks. He wanted very little from life, other than to practice his swordsmanship.

The mood in the city was subdued. People still talked and laughed, but it was becoming rarer. There was a sense that something bad was about to happen.

'How were the protests last night?' Alex asked, as they walked along the street.

'Loud!' Carlos replied. 'They've requisitioned the last part of City Park. The whole thing's going to Fortrillium. There'll be no park left now.'

The conversation was brought to an end as Alex spotted their friend ahead.

'Hey, Deena. How's things?'

A shy-looking girl wearing a plain grey beanie and matching mittens joined them from her perch on a wall outside a coffee shop.

'No coffee today, guys, just green tea. Sorry!'

'Jeez, we'll be drinking cabbage water next!' said Carlos.

'Yeah, they're out and they're not sure if any more is coming in. Apparently they're prioritizing essential imports – and that doesn't include coffee.'

'Well, tea it is!' Alex took one of the covered cardboard cups.

As they approached the VaXX centre, they could see dozens of people patiently waiting their turn. Alex turned inward as they joined the back of the queue. He didn't want to catch Harley's gaze. Too late. Harley had seen Deena and he knew they travelled as a group.

'Hey, Brady, pity they haven't got a VaXX programme for idiots yet!'

It was always the same with Harley. He used to be a pal,

but ever since he'd joined Fortrillium's Youth Wing, he'd changed into an arrogant bully.

'Hi guys!' Simone called out.

Simone was a bridge between them. She knew that Harley was being a jerk, but hoped he'd come out of it one day. That day didn't look like it was coming soon.

This was college life now. They seemed to spend as much time waiting in queues as they did getting educated. It wasn't entirely clear who was ordering it – Fortrillium or the President's office. There was a lot that wasn't clear these days.

'You know, I'm thinking of skipping this one,' Carlos suddenly announced.

Deena was shocked.

'You can't do that, Carlos.'

'None of us likes it, man, but we've got to do it,' Alex joined in. 'You know what happens if you don't. Think of it like one of Deena's software updates. Every now and then we all need an upgrade. And they're getting tougher. I heard a woman got shot in our block last week. Shot! It's scary, I'm having mine.'

'It's a conspiracy, I'm telling you!' Carlos said, hushed so that only his friends could hear. 'My dad reckons Fortrillium will take the farm. They'll put it under state control, and then what'll we do? How will we live? And these VaXX programs, what are they about? They say they're to keep us safe, but look what happened to Audra ...'

Carlos looked at Alex and knew that he'd pushed it too far. Deena squeezed Alex's arm, she could see his eyes were filling with tears. They always did when Audra was mentioned.

'We don't know what happened to her!'

Alex instantly regretted his outburst.

'I'm sorry, but you've got to cool it, Carlos. Audra knew what she was doing with her tech, and there's no way they could have detected her. I don't know what happened to her, but I'm certain it wasn't anything to do with Fortrillium.'

'Are we going in?' Deena asked. The queue had moved along and it was almost their turn.

'How long do we have to take this one?' Alex asked.

'By Monday. If you're not up-to-date with the latest programme by 18:00 hours, you're in trouble.'

Deena always had a grasp of the detail. It was why she was so good with her laptop. She and Audra had always been way ahead of the boys when it came to tech. Carlos was useless, he was an offline kind of a guy. Swords and self-sufficiency were his thing, preparing for an apocalypse that until recently had seemed just a fantasy.

Deena and Audra had been friends since meeting in the children's home as orphaned ten-year-olds. Alex knew Deena felt her friend's loss as badly as he did, but she kept quiet about it. She coped with things on her own.

'Easy!' Harley emerged from the VaXX unit, smirking. 'That's me up with the programme. Hope you guys aren't going to chicken out.'

Simone joined them, anxious to defuse the tension.

'Hi everyone. It's quite a deep needle this one, sorry.'

She tried to keep things genial. She'd like to have hung out more with the crew, but the way Harley had been behaving, it was difficult. Harley was working his way up at Fortrillium, they liked him. She daren't rock the boat.

They walked off together.

'I'm going to give this one a miss,' Alex said. 'I'll get it done tomorrow. I need some time on my own. Is that okay guys?'

Deena nodded. Carlos stepped aside with him.

'Me too. I'm going to skip this one permanently, see what happens. You sure you don't want some company?'

Alex shook his head. He'd been thinking about Audra. He wanted to go to their special place.

He said his goodbyes to his friends and headed along the avenue towards City Park. He generally tried to stay away from the area. You could never tell when more violence would erupt there. But the tree at the side of the bridge had been their place. There'd been no body to bury, so he'd placed a Memory Tab there. Only his friends and Audra's parents knew of its existence.

He was shocked by how much the park had changed since he'd last been there a month ago. Fortrillium had needed bespoke headquarters to manage security and municipal administration after the state borders were closed and City Park was the ideal location. But it hadn't been without controversy. Protesters gathered there all the time, but they were moved on and some disappeared without a trace. The project continued, relentless in its scope and progress. Day by day the structure got bigger. Soon it would take over the whole of the park.

Alex walked along the path and climbed down the muddy bank to reach their tree. It had been their private place where they'd sit and talk for hours. They were right in the heart of a huge city, but felt as if they were miles from anywhere. He placed his finger on the Memory Tab, which he'd embedded into the trunk of the tree. It authenticated him immediately and the montage of Audra's life began to play.

He'd compiled this footage with Deena's help, using video archive of their time together. It felt like only yesterday that Audra had been there beside him. The city had changed drastically since she'd gone. She'd barely recognize it now.

He could recite the words from the video clips, he'd watched this montage so many times. He felt choked as the final photographs scrolled through and faded to black, the last image one of them walking through that very park and kicking the autumn leaves. That area was Fortrillium property now, as this section would soon become too.

He waited for the Memory Tab to switch itself off, but it didn't move on to its usual deactivation process. Instead, it switched to a new video, which had been roughly added to the end. A face came onto the screen. It was Audra, but not Audra as he knew her. Her hair was cut short to the scalp and her right eye covered with a patch. She spoke urgently, as if she expected to be interrupted at any moment.

'Alex ... Deena ... whichever one of you sees this. I'm alive. They've got me. Fortrillium. They knew what I was doing all along. It's horrible here. I can't take it much longer. Ask for Jasmine Haworth. But be careful. Please, be careful. If they catch you, you'll end up here with me. I love you ... I knew you'd come here. Please help—'

She looked to her side, then abruptly ended the video recording.

Alex sat there and wept.

CHAPTER TWO

———————

'He really has no idea we're able to do this?'

'None whatsoever, Mr Kincade. There's no way he can trace it.'

Bryce Kincade already had James Morgan marked out for better things. The man was ambitious. He understood Fortrillium's role in the future of their state, and he'd leaped at the chance to become a part of the organization. It was already paying off.

A series of muffled sounds were running through an audio feed, routed via Morgan's console. It was the distinctive voice of Shane Scorsese, Fortrillium's most vociferous opponent. He was making his breakfast. Every now and then his voice could be heard giving an instruction to his digital assistant.

'Surya – Channel 9 news – low volume.'

In the background a flat screen activated and the stream of audio from the latest news bulletin could be heard at Morgan's desk.

'Surya – diary – today's appointments.'

The reassuring computer-generated voice read out a list of that day's commitments.

09:00 *Meeting with President Lance Henderson. Topic: Encroachment of Fortrillium activities in City Park area. Location: President's residence. Note: Access level 10 required.*

10:15 *Meeting with Deena Jakobson. Location: TBC ...*

Kincade smiled. It worked like a dream.

'So, how is the surveillance initiative going, Morgan?'

'We have a 95 per cent penetration into your watch list, sir. It's amazing how much people trust these things.'

Digital assistants had become an essential part of domestic routines in the early twenty-first century. Now they were providing a highly effective web of surveillance for Fortrillium. Using Morgan's unparalleled skills with technology, Kincade had set up an audio keyword monitoring system, which could be directly routed to the devices. While Fortrillium's opponents thought they could plot against the sinister organization in private, in truth, government had won the right to monitor their feeds several years before the troubles began. It only took a sleight of hand with the legislature for Kincade to have all the access he needed.

He watched as Morgan's screen highlighted the words *President Lance Henderson* and *Deena Jakobson,* extracted the audio and added it to an alerts file.

'This Jakobson girl – woman – she's come up before, hasn't she?'

'Yes, but we've nothing on her. It seems she's meeting Scorsese to discuss an accommodation issue. Something to do with power outages due to the construction works in the City Park area. There's nothing in their conversations that's raised any flags yet. You want me to move her up a level?'

Kincade thought it through. It was always the youngsters that caused the most fuss when it came to the deletions. An old biddy like Rose Kingston was forgotten in no time. People like that were kept afloat by their influence, not by friendship. As many people were pleased to see the back of her as were concerned by her disappearance. Besides, they'd got the message. Create too much of a fuss and you'll end up like Senator Kingston: gone without a trace, your property requisitioned by Fortrillium. Nobody wanted that.

'Where is she with the VaXX programme? Has she taken it yet?'

Morgan switched to a second, smaller console and entered Deena's surname and forename.

'No, she registered but missed her appointment.'

'How about Scorsese? I bet that little toad hasn't updated his yet.'

Again, Morgan interrogated the data on his screen.

'The usual protest, sir. He's scheduled in an appointment five minutes before the Monday deadline. But he has scheduled it.'

'That's because he knows he's skating on thin ice. The minute he's active, I want you to mark him for deletion. Nothing too soon, but within two weeks I want him gone. I'm tempted to take him out with a bullet in the good old-fashioned way, but in his case, I think that might be a little too obvious. In fact, it's my birthday on the twenty-second. Mark it for then. It will be a lovely present to wake up to.'

Morgan tapped away at the screen, adding Scorsese to an already long list of names.

'I like you, Morgan. You're exactly what we need at Fortrillium: people who see the future and who understand the way things have to be. I see big things ahead of you. You're an asset to our state. Not long now and your life is going to change forever.'

'Thank you, sir.'

Morgan had every intention of following the trajectory that Kincade had alluded to. He had worked his way through Fortrillium and learned its secrets. Still a young man, he'd already achieved more than he could have imagined when he was stuck working in the Federal Civil Service. Morgan could see the change that was coming and he was going to ride it. Just like Kincade.

Kincade's Comms device sounded.

'That's my meeting with the President. He always calls them early – I'm sure it's a control thing. I'd better get him warmed up for his 9 o'clock with Scorsese. This is good work, Morgan. Keep me informed.'

Kincade strode off, nodding to some of the other workers at their stations. Things were coming together at last. Soon Fortrillium would have full control of the city and surrounding territory. First, though, there was Henderson to deal with.

President Lance Henderson was old school. For Bryce Kincade, that meant he was a pain in the neck. As the first President of Sector 4 to be appointed under the emergency constitutional changes, Henderson was finding the transition from Mayor to be a difficult one. He was elderly and he was popular, as popular as a government official could ever be. And that gave Kincade a problem. If only he could delete Henderson and hand over his powers to someone a little more friendly. It would be a fast and sudden coup. But under the newly defined constitution, Fortrillium was subject to the authority of the President.

Kincade still had maneuvers to make to change the balance of power. It would begin with the assembly of his own peacekeeping force. That's what he'd call them at first. The disorder generated by the agitators he'd paid to stir up trouble at City Park would ensure he got his funding. And when he could outgun Henderson, he'd take the old man down.

'Mr President, it's good to see you!'

He strode into the office, stretching out his hand towards the President as if they were the best of friends.

'Good morning, Mr Kincade. Thanks for agreeing to this early meeting. I have to be mindful of the time, I'm afraid. I'm seeing Shane Scorsese at nine. I need you to brief me on this recruitment drive that you're after. To be honest with you, I'm a bit concerned—'

'Let me stop you there, Mr President. I'm guessing that Scorsese has been whispering in your ear about police states and the like? It's a compelling view, I understand that, and I can see why you're worried. This new system of government is unfamiliar to all of us, we're very much feeling our way. But you saw what happened on the border overnight?'

'Yes, I most certainly did.'

Of course he knew about it. Kincade had paid a group of local mobsters to raze the President's old community church to the ground. If that didn't work, they'd be heading for the family store next. It was still run by the President's sister. That'd help him to focus his mind.

'It's very troubling, Kincade. This state-line unrest, it seems to be getting worse. A lot of the other states are struggling, I know. But this is how we agreed to deal with our issues. It's enshrined in the legislature. We have to enforce the boundaries.'

'The new force will be recruited and trained personally by Richter. You know his record. He's a patriot, sir. It was his leadership which brought the Korean conflict to an end—'

'Yes, and left it a wasteland!'

'You know it was always insoluble, sir. But Richter puts the interests of his country before himself, and now it's his state that he's putting first. He's the best man for the job. If you want to be in with a chance of being the last state standing, it has to be this way.'

'I agree that we need something stronger than the police, as powerful as the army, but they have to be under my rule. That must not slip away from me.'

'Understood, sir. But can I get your permission to begin the recruitment programme? Richter is ready. He's drawn up a target list for those he wants in the key positions.'

Kincade handed the President the portable screen on which he'd pulled up a list of names. Henderson scrutinized them, then looked up, handing back the device.

'I'll let you go ahead with this recruitment, but they must be answerable to me, not Fortrillium. And I want the paperwork drawn up by the legal department: no active operations until it's completed – understood?'

Kincade nodded, hiding a smirk. He'd got what he'd come for. Richter would assemble his own military unit, recruiting the best of the best. Under Kincade's direction, another incident would be engineered in the President's hometown requiring their deployment before there was time to sort out the paperwork. That would give Kincade his remit to activate the force, and the precedent would be set. After that nobody would stop him. As long as he delivered a reasonable quota of public-pleasing missions, Kincade and his new militia would be free to work in the shadows.

'And what will I tell Mr Scorsese?' the President asked, getting up from his seat. 'He won't like this.'

'Shane Scorsese doesn't like anything we do. That's the way he's wired. Tell him it's about securing the state border, keeping our residents safe. Reassure him on the legalities.

But I wouldn't worry too much about Mr Scorsese. I suspect he may soon be retiring from politics.'

———

'Are you home, Mum?'

Alex couldn't decide whether or not he should tell her about the video in the Memory Tab. While he was thinking about it, he noticed there was a letter from his dad on the table. It had a red stamp across the back of the envelope. It was over three months old, according to the date at the top. *Opened in the interests of state security.* That was nothing new when it came to receiving letters from Area 9 Correctional. Alex missed his dad. Michael Brady was being held on remand, at the same time as the legislature was going down the pan. All trials were on a long delay – he'd been in there almost nine months already.

'Alex? One moment ... I've just come out of the shower. The water ran cold again. This city is falling apart, I swear!'

Alex ran his eyes over the letter. It was the usual stuff. An apology. A declaration of innocence. A few words about how he missed them and how he'd be out soon. Area 9 Correctional was supposed to have been closed down at the beginning of the century, but there was no chance of that now. He sighed. Bit by bit, things were changing. None of the changes were good. It was incremental, like the shower water not being hot, a series of little things making life more difficult by the day.

Susan Brady's badge was on the table next to the letter. It was ironic. There was his mum, a senior firearms officer and upholder of the law, and his dad was incarcerated in that rotting tip of a prison. Harley loved to remind him of that.

'Hi, Alex, you saw the letter then?'

Susan Brady was wearing jeans and a grey sweatshirt, her uniform hung up for another day. She was Mum now, not the head of the city's Strategic Response Group. You wouldn't have known her status by looking at their modest apartment. It was on the eleventh floor and the lifts were always breaking down. It could take days for them to be repaired. The legal costs involved with his father's case meant they'd had to take a big financial hit.

'Do you think we'll ever get him out of there, Mum? It's going to be a year soon. The same with Audra.'

Susan hesitated, darting a worried look at her son.

'What is it?'

'I took that job, Alex.'

'Wow! I didn't think you would.'

'I couldn't refuse it. Truth be told, I'm terrified. But if I'd turned it down, things would get much worse for us. You do see that?'

Alex nodded. They were all having to do things they didn't want to.

'When do you start?'

'I've started already.'

Alex was surprised by that.

'They don't hang about.'

'It's the last time I'll wear my badge and uniform. All these years and it ends like this.'

'I hope you're not going to look like that creepy Richter guy on the flat screens – all that black. He's scary.'

'It was him I spoke to today. You know he's a war hero? I guess if you'd served in that war in Korea, you'd have to be tough.'

'And you're still head of firearms?'

'Yes, same post, different organization. It's Fortrillium paying the rent now, not the city's police force.'

'Mum ...'

He wanted to tell her about Audra. For a moment, the words were there, but he pulled back. He had to be careful what he told her.

'There's home mum and work mum,' she'd say.

If he told her about Carlos's collection of deadly swords, she'd have to warn him that they were regulated items and that Carlos was not permitted to use them in an unsupervised environment. It was the curse of having a family member in the city's police force, just one of life's bummers.

'Do you think your new job will mean you can help Dad?'

Alex asked the question that was the second thing on his mind after Audra's message.

'It can't hurt him. I'll get to meet Bryce Kincade and I'll petition him for Dad's case to be fast-tracked. That's what tipped me over the edge into saying yes to the job. The extra money will be good too. We need the income.'

'I could quit college and help out?'

Susan held up her hand.

'I won't hear of it! You need qualifications. Things are only going to get worse. I want you out of all this, working in some nice office somewhere.'

Alex nodded. He had no aspirations to follow in his mother's footsteps. She was the practical member of the household. It was Susan who fixed the plumbing, Susan who mended the sockets, and Susan who adjusted the appliances. Like his father, Alex thought the best kind of job involved sitting in a comfortable chair and working at a terminal. The safer, the better.

Only, it was precisely that which had got his father into

trouble. 'Misappropriation of Cryptocurrency' was how the charges read. It was an easy stitch-up, according to Deena, but Alex hadn't really understood it. He was more a games environment kind of guy when it came to tech.

'I have to be out of the house early tomorrow, so you won't see me in the morning. It's a 05:00 hours start at Fortrillium for me. I'm part of the escort team for Jasmine Haworth—'

Alex looked up at her, startled.

'What? You look like I told you I'm going to shoot you.'

Was this a home mum, work mum situation? Now Susan worked for Fortrillium, he'd have to get a sense of how the land was lying. He played innocent.

'Oh nothing. It's just that I heard her name mentioned on the flat screen the other day. Who is she, some big shot?'

'She's one of our best chances of beating this flu outbreak: Professor Jasmine Haworth, Head of Disease and Immunology at Magnum Enterprises. That's what the briefing sheet says. They've built her a laboratory at Fortrillium; she's one of the only people who have been allowed to fly cross-state into City Airport. She must be pretty important if Sector 15 let her go.'

'Why does she need an armed escort?'

'It's vital she's delivered securely inside Fortrillium. She's key to everything. It would be a disaster if anything happened to her.'

'Where's she going to be tomorrow, this Professor Haworth? Which entrance are you taking her into?'

'Come on, Alex. You know I can't give you times and locations. Why do you want to know? How come you're so interested in her?'

'No reason, just trying to stay informed. Things are changing so quickly in the city, it's difficult to keep up.'

It can't have been a coincidence. One minute Audra was telling him to speak to this woman, the next his own mother was smuggling her into the city. There was no way Alex was ignoring Audra's plea for help.

It would be an early start for both him and his mum. She was going to protect a high value asset, and he was going to get as close to Jasmine Haworth as he could. Audra was alive. He loved her. And he was going to find out where they were keeping her.

Deena had warned Alex not to go ahead, but he was adamant. So, putting aside her reservations, she helped him deliver on his crazy plan.

Just forward this text update to your mum's work device. The scan won't detect it. You can track her when she's inside the city limits. You'll have a short window to get to which-ever entrance they're using. How's your running?

Alex and Deena had something in common: they were both in love with Audra. But Deena's love was unrequited. She'd been close to Audra – really close – but like sisters. Audra only had eyes for Alex, Deena understood that, and if she'd been into men, she'd have fallen for Alex too. He was a good guy. With Alex around she felt close to Audra. It was as if he had her smell on her.

You want me to come with you?

Deena had set up a secure system in a dark area which she and her friends could use without fear of being discov-ered. She knew better than to send text messages between devices. You never knew who was listening in.

I'm good, thanks. Appreciate your help, Deena. Wish me luck. If I screw up, at least I'll get to be with my dad again.

Deena had a meeting of her own. She'd already spoken to Scorsese the day before, in person and in a busy part of the city, where she was safe. She'd reached out to him, spinning some yarn about power outages in her block. She'd seen what he'd done at City Park. Shane Scorsese seemed to be a politician who genuinely cared.

She was nervous walking across the city so late at night. Carlos had told her many a time that she needed to change her body language.

'Everything about you screams "victim", Deena.'

'This is just how I am,' she'd reply. 'I can't do anything about it, Carlos.'

He'd sigh, hug her and reassure her that she only need call him if she ever needed his help.

Deena thought about the project she'd been working on with Audra. They'd been trying to hack into the Fortrillium network. From time to time, as the girls had plotted together, Deena allowed herself to hope there might be something between them after all. But then Audra would start to talk about Alex, and Deena had to accept it was only a fantasy.

They had agreed that Alex must never know what they were doing – he was such a coward, he'd tell them to stop. Besides, his mother's job made it impossible to involve him. They must have been onto something. She was certain of it. Why else had Audra disappeared? And now she was going to share what they had discovered with Shane Scorsese, for better or for worse.

'Fancy seeing you out at this time of night. What are you up to?'

It was Harley Lydell, uniformed in black. And armed. He had a companion, another sneering youth, eyeing her up and trying to figure out what kind of a girl she was.

'Damn it, Harley. You scared the life out of me!'

'Hey, pretty!' Harley's mate grinned.

Deena took a step back, but Harley moved into the vacated space.

'Night-time training patrols,' he explained, not that she'd asked. 'They're giving us more responsibility each day. We're on the lookout for suspicious activity. Which brings me back to you, Deena.'

'I needed some air,' Deena began, aware that Harley's chum was working his way round to her side. They were trying to corner her, closing in on her. Her stomach was churning. She had to get away.

'What's in the bag?' Harley asked. 'Want to check it, Phil?'

Deena clasped the strap of her rucksack. What was it Carlos had said about body language? She tried to make herself seem bigger, but failed miserably. She heard Phil snigger. He placed his hand on her behind. Deena could barely recall what happened next. One minute he was attempting to touch her, the next he was on the floor with a bloody nose.

Harley stepped back, they hadn't expected this.

Deena's heart was beating furiously. She was terrified of what they'd do next. There was a pause.

'You stupid bitch. What the hell do you think you're doing?' Phil yelled, a string of blood and mucus dangling from his nose.

It was the last thing they'd expected her to do.

'Deena doesn't behave the same as the other girls, if you know what I mean!' Harley chipped in, taking a step back.

She'd heard it all before, she'd survived high school, hadn't she? The other kids had figured out there was something about her and boys quite young, before she even really understood it herself. So she was used to the language. Nobody had ever gone as far as this, though.

Harley looked at his friend, and then at Deena. She was scared, yes, but he could see she was ready to fight.

'Come on, Phil. Let's leave this weirdo alone. She's not worth the trouble.'

He lurched towards her, but only to scare her. It was an attempt to win back some control. Deena pulled her bag tight against her back and sprinted away. This was the future. Teenage boys with uniforms and power. It would bring out the worst in them.

She ran as fast as she could, avoiding the main roads, weaving her way through alleys and back streets. She was as certain as she could be that she hadn't been followed. Before she entered Scorsese's block, she sat on a bench across from the high rise and used her phone to run a sweep for cameras. There was one in the hallway and a street cam. She disabled both.

Deena waited for one of the residents to enter the building. She slipped in behind him, catching the door before it clicked back onto the lock. The man took the lift, so Deena ducked into the staircase. She didn't want anyone other than Scorsese to know she'd been there. It was being careless that had got Audra caught.

Scorsese was on the seventh floor. Deena wasn't unfit but she was out of breath by the time she reached his door. Apartment 9, Floor 7, that's what he'd told her. She knocked, quietly, not wanting to encourage any of his neighbours out onto the landing. She heard shuffling from inside – and another voice.

She wasn't expecting him to have company. She considered running. Was this a set-up? Had Scorsese tipped off

Fortrillium? He was a politician, after all, and they were all scumbags at heart – weren't they?

It was too late, he was opening the door.

'Deena, come in.'

Scorsese checked along the corridor, making sure that she hadn't been followed.

'You can never be too careful. Fortrillium has eyes and ears everywhere. They're going to have this entire state on lockdown soon.'

'Who else have you got in there? You didn't say you'd have anyone with you. I told you, this is highly sensitive information. I have to know that I can trust you.'

'It's fine, Deena. I wasn't expecting him, but I couldn't turn him away. Not once I heard his story. You'll want to hear what he has to say too. It pertains to our own conversation.'

Deena followed Scorsese into the living room, reluctant and cautious.

'This is Evan Price. He's been serving on the border patrols, and he has quite a story to tell.'

CHAPTER THREE

Bryce Kincade allowed himself a moment of pride as he contemplated the astonishing achievement that was the construction of Fortrillium's huge new underground prison. As an infrastructure project it was amazing, considering the short time it had taken to build the empty shell under the river. Located between Phoenix Tunnel and Quantum Bridge, the new facility ran almost adjacent to what had once been City Park.

Morgan had convinced him to carry out its construction covertly, overriding his original plan to use the existing network of tunnels and railways. As he had put it, they didn't want to scare the horses. And he was right. For such a young man, he had an uncanny ability to anticipate the outcome of certain actions. So far, the prison had been built in total secrecy, using convicts as laborers. Only a select few knew that it existed.

The walls around the state border would come next, and once they went up, there would be no hiding it from the outside world any longer. It would be there for all to see. They were creating a fortress.

The prison would be used to house the horde of dissenters, criminals and killers that would surface when things got really serious. There would be a flood of refugees too, fleeing from the ravages of the virus if it finally beat their efforts to control it. They'd make their way into Sector 4 and, no doubt, there would be some residents who would wish to leave it. Either way, they would be bricked in eventually. A physical barrier would be the only way to survive. There would be some alliances, of course, but Sector 4 was well placed to survive and under Kincade's leadership he would make sure that it did.

The first concrete pillars of the vast wall had been sunk along the state boundary. That work had started the previous month, and it was progressing well. But this visit was to mark the completion of their most ambitious project to date: the huge underground prison that would inevitably be required if the endgame began to play out.

The prison was a short shuttle ride from the main Fortrillium building. Security was tight, with armed guards at every turn. Richter had made certain that his instructions had been followed. Bryce wondered why it had taken the threat of annihilation to get a facility like this built. He blamed all the talk of human rights and democracy, which got in the way of progress. This place would hold society's unwanted. And, if his influence continued to grow in the way he anticipated, it would also be home to his most vociferous political opponents.

The stench of sweat and excrement struck him as he passed through the final security gate and into the main dome of the prison. He was greeted by a man in a white coat, a coat that was as white as his beard.

'What do you think, Labatt? Can you make this work?'

The old man surveyed the vast underground cavern and smiled.

'Once we have Haworth in place, yes, we can make it work. Mind you, it would be useful if you stopped killing off your opponents. Leave some alive for me.'

The men laughed.

'How many in here now?'

'Five hundred so far – the first contingent from Area 9 Correctional. We're shipping them out slowly, but we're still having problems with the press. I assume you're onto that?'

'Yes, I am, but it's difficult – after so many years of free speech they're used to challenging authority and asking questions. I'm taking a more diplomatic approach to that one. Bribery and societal advantage. It'll have to do until the latest VaXX programme is completed.'

More laughter. It was a collusion of sociopaths.

A voice called out from behind the cold metal bars of a cell.

'Hey, Kincade, you know you can't hide this forever!'

There was a buzz of discontent from the other inmates.

'Is that Brady? Does that man never shut up?' Kincade asked.

A flash of anger crossed his face.

'Don't worry, his time will soon be up,' said Labatt.

'Well, don't rush things. His wife is important to me. She's a very capable woman. It's just a shame she's got so much integrity. I'll have a word with him.'

As Kincade approached the cell, the smell got worse. It was sweat, blood and any other disgusting mess that could flow out of a human being. The cells were two rows high, but they could expand upwards if they needed to. There was no segregation here. Men were incarcerated with women, pensioners with their teenage counterparts.

'Brady, good to see you. How's that appeal coming on? I see you're still with us.'

He sneered at Michael Brady, openly displaying his disgust at his dirty hair and filthy clothing. It had taken this strategic internment to get his wife to agree to join Fortrillium. Kincade had been courting her for months, and it was only that day that she'd signed her contract. At every turn he'd held out the hope of her husband's release. Well, more fool her. She'd taken the latest VaXX shot and signed her pact with the devil. Susan Brady's soul was now his.

'You're a monster, Kincade! I've got a son out there who needs me. And my wife, does she have any idea what you're doing here? This is against our human rights.'

Kincade laughed, genuinely amused at his naivety.

'Now you're here, Brady, you have no human rights. You're surplus to requirements. We're giving you a new job working with Dr Labatt. I'm sure you'll enjoy it. It'll be of great service to that son of yours, and your wife. In the meantime, you stink. The lot of you do.

'Don't we have a way to clean this place?' he continued, to nobody in particular. 'I'd like to see it in action!'

Labatt smiled again and gave his reply.

'You'd better stand back, it's very powerful when it's in operation.'

Kincade followed Julius Labatt into the safety of an enclosure set behind reinforced glass doors. As the door closed behind them, he could hear the rowdy discontent of the inmates. They knew what was coming. They'd experienced it once before, just after their transfer. From the top of the domed roof, great sheets of water crashed down from outlets in the ceiling, gushing through the cages, pinning the screaming prisoners inside to the floor.

Kincade and Labatt continued chatting. They showed no emotion at the atrocity that was going on beyond the protective glass.

'I've decided there's no point delaying any longer, Julius. As soon as Haworth gets here I want the trials to begin. We need to start shipping them out of Area 9 Correctional much faster now. You have my blessing to start work.'

'Thank you, Bryce. I'm certain we'll make a break-through soon. And if Haworth plays ball, they'll soon be hailing you as the savior of humanity.'

Kincade smiled to himself as he watched the flow of water coming to an end and the inmates struggling to their feet, relieved their immediate misery was over. Until the next time.

'You know, I've just thought of a great name for this place. We should call it "The Soak".'

Deena scanned the room. At that moment, she wasn't interested in Evan Price. She knew what she was looking for, and a man like Scorsese, with no family and cash to spare, was bound to have one.

The apartment could be described as minimalist. The sparse furnishings were tasteful and clearly expensive. Scorsese might portray himself as a man of the people, but there were always advantages to be had in a position of power.

'Let's get down to business,' he began.

Deena placed her finger to her lips and frowned at him.

He looked at her, alarmed by the look of concern on her face.

She placed her bag on the sofa and began a closer inspection of shelves and surfaces. It wasn't long before she found what she'd been looking for.

'It's a Model 13. That must have set you back a bit. What do you call it?'

Scorsese's face reddened.

'Surya ... it's my wife's name. My former—'

'I don't need to know. Deactivate her please. Deactivate it.'

'Surya, deactivate.'

Surya deactivating. Do you require me to reactivate at a predesignated time?

Deena shook her head.

'No, Surya, deactivate until further notice.' He hesitated before adding, 'Goodnight.'

He looked sheepish.

'It's not alive,' said Deena. 'It's just a load of electronics. I'll bet that's your wife's voice too. She sounds nice. But it's not her, you need to realize that. It has no conscience and no morals. It will betray you without a thought.'

'I'm guessing you've never been in love?'

It was Deena's turn to fight off a red face.

'If you had been, you'd understand.'

'I'm sorry. It's just that they listen through these things. We're supposed to be protected by privacy laws, but everything's changing. Fortrillium is no force for good. They're not here to educate our children and look after our environment. They're ruthless. They will do whatever it takes to ensure their survival.'

Scorsese looked at her, surprised at the articulate outburst from such a diminutive, introverted young woman.

For the first time, Evan spoke.

'She's right, Mr Scorsese. I've seen some terrible things at the borders. Troops shot for daring to criticize Fortrillium's actions. Farmers hanged because they held back some of their crops to sell on the Black Market. The flat screens would have you believe that everything is okay. It's not. They're scared. They're closing borders, restricting movement, bringing in state autocracies. You can't trust Fortrillium. I told you what they did to my family …'

His voice shook and his eyes filled with tears. Deena was unsure of how to respond to his emotional outburst. Scorsese moved towards him and squeezed his arm.

'This thing isn't even commercial. It's been adapted,' Deena said, setting straight to work on Surya.

'I told you, it's my wife's voice. I had to get all my videos of her digitized so that the voice could be recreated. It has her mannerisms and intonation too. Surely you can forgive me that indulgence?'

'I'm not judging you, Mr Scorsese.'

Deena's concern about his tech had come over as being hard-hearted. She knew what it was like to lose someone she loved, but he'd been careless. He needed to heed the warnings about what was going on.

'They've been monitoring you. Didn't you know that?'

Scorsese turned around. She could see that he realized how naive he'd been.

'No, I didn't know. I have anti-interference software on it, and I thought that was enough. Are you sure it's been hacked? How?'

Deena held up the unit to show him – as if he'd understand. She'd prized off the bottom to reveal the electronics inside.

'It's enabled for listening. You can tell because somebody has built in a bridging system. There's probably some civil servant listening in right this minute.'

As if to illustrate the point, she shouted, 'Hello! Are you enjoying yourself snooping in on people's private conversations? You should be ashamed of yourself!'

'Is it safe now?' Scorsese asked. His apartment was regularly swept for bugs, but he hadn't even considered that Surya could be used as a listening device. He recoiled when he thought of what they might have heard: confidential conversations, plots and plans. Nothing that would condemn him under normal circumstances, but now? Who could tell?

'We need to get out of here,' Deena said. 'We can't talk in your apartment, it's not safe. They'll be monitoring your phone too.'

'Mr Scorsese, I'm thinking back to our conversation before Deena arrived,' Price said, his voice much steadier now. 'I told you that Fortrillium had taken my family, and then I said I was going to kill that monster, Richter. I think I might have shown my hand. They'll call me a traitor.'

As if on cue, the reflections of flashing lights on the street below lit up the apartment. Car doors were being slammed.

Deena walked to the window and looked down. They were not so high up that she couldn't see what was going on.

'It's Richter's thugs. They're entering the building. They might be coming for someone else, not us.'

'I'm not sure I want to hang around to find out,' said Evan. 'Is there any way out of here?'

Scorsese looked around, as if he was going to find the answer in the apartment.

'There are two sets of stairs and two lifts, that's it. Apart from the helipad on the roof, there's no other way out.'

'Think about maintenance crews, building work, stuff like that. There must be another way down,' said Deena.

Scorsese was only seven floors up and she knew they had to think fast.

'There's a chute for building debris on floor five, but there's no way I'm going down that. It'd be suicide.'

For a few seconds no one spoke. Price was a soldier, he knew how these things played out.

'I'm with Deena. If they heard our conversation, they'll come for us.'

'We won't have any options soon,' said Deena. 'Let's go.'

They left the apartment and walked into the corridor. She moved towards the stairwell.

'We have to reach floor five before they do, and we've got a two-floor start on them. Come on, hurry!'

As she spoke, there was a ping and the doors of the lift further along the corridor started to open. Deena had her hand on the door to the stairwell and Evan was behind her, but Scorsese was dithering outside the apartment entrance, unsure about fleeing the scene.

Two armed men stepped out of the lift. They were clad top-to-toe in black. These were not the local police.

'Shane Scorsese, ref: MK88, you're required to accompany us for questioning on suspicion of counter-state activities. Kneel down and put your hands on your head.'

The colour drained from Scorsese's face. He couldn't believe what was happening. He looked at the Troopers, assessing their weapons, and then turned towards Deena and Evan. He was closer to the landing door than he was to the lifts. The men sensed what he was thinking and raised their guns.

He ran faster than he'd ever run before. They began to

fire, chunks of plaster flying off the walls and blinding him with puffs of dust.

'They're coming up the staircase. Hurry!' Deena shouted.

'I can't see! My eyes, they're full of plaster.'

'Take my arm!'

Through the window she could see more Troopers on the ground below. They were running towards the door of the stairwell. Their colleagues must be at floor two or even three now.

'Are you sure it's floor five?'

They began to move down the staircase, the sound of heavy boots thundering towards them.

'No! I got that wrong. It can't be floor five – every fifth floor is coloured red from the outside. It has to be floor six, the one below me.'

'We're here now, come on, hold tight to me.'

'They're just below us,' Evan said, looking over the handrail. 'We have to move now.'

Footsteps were approaching from above and below. It had to be floor six or they were out of time.

'Where is it? Where is the chute?' Deena was scanning the corridor.

'Move towards the middle, opposite the lift doors.'

They could hear the Troopers approaching. They were assembling at either end of the corridor. Radios were crackling, a plan of attack being communicated, weapons readied. They charged along the corridor.

'This is it!' Deena cried.

In front of them was a security barrier covered in safety notices. In the middle of it was a locked door. Evan clocked the lift moving up through the floors. It had reached level four. They had no time to spare. He took out the gun concealed inside his jacket and fired three times, shattering the padlock. He kicked the door open.

In the middle of the room was a rough wooden table. Strewn over it was a collection of plans, weighted down with lumps of rubble. A selection of workmen's tools were ranged by the far wall. Secured to what was left of the window frame was the large opening to a plastic funnel.

'There's the chute. We haven't any choice,' Deena cried.

'There's no way I'm going down that thing!' Scorsese shouted at her, frantically wiping his eyes, trying to regain full vision.

There was a shot along the corridor, then a burst of automated gunfire.

'You've got to go down it or you'll end up like my friend Audra. Now move!'

Deena climbed onto the window frame and threw herself down the chute. Evan was up next. He waited a moment, giving her enough time to roll out of the way when she reached the bottom. Who knew what would be waiting for them in the skip below? He looked at Scorsese, and then launched himself off the window frame through the neck of the giant tube.

Moments later, the Troopers burst in, fingers on triggers ready to shoot. They were too late. All they saw was the head of politician and people's representative Shane Scorsese disappearing down a plastic builder's chute from a height of six floors up.

Alex waited until Susan Brady had left the house. She was early. It was a little after four o'clock when she opened his bedroom door to whisper her goodbyes, to tell him she loved him. He played the sleeping teenager. He didn't want to give her an inkling of what he was planning. Since his father had left, she'd become much more protective. He knew what she was doing to keep the family together. But he had to find Audra.

Alex ran through the timings. His mum had said they were picking up Professor Jasmine Haworth from City Airport. No passenger aircraft flew in or out of the airport any more. The only planes they saw were military jets. It had been like that for little over a year. They'd probably get to Fortrillium by seven, so Alex reckoned he needed to be there an hour earlier. Morning traffic was still heavy; life was going on in the city almost as normal.

Alex considered what he was about to do. It would create some discomfort for his mum. He wished she'd delayed taking the job a bit longer. But in spite of Deena and Carlos's conspiracy theories, and his own distress over Audra's disappearance, Alex was still convinced that there was nothing sinister about Fortrillium. His own mother had accepted a job there, and she was a highly respected member of the law enforcement community, and an expert in her field. She wouldn't have signed up with Fortrillium if they were up to no good. He was certain his friends had got it wrong. Times were changing, sure, but Fortrillium was there to protect them.

He wondered if Carlos would be awake. He knew his friend was an early riser. All that sword stuff required patience and tenacity.

Alex decided to send him a text message.

Heading to City Park/Fortrillium. Fancy an adventure? Join me. I'll explain it when you get there.

He watched as the message was received, then read, but Carlos didn't reply. It was still early and he was probably playing dead, much as Alex had with his mum earlier on.

Alex scratched around the kitchen in search of something to eat. He couldn't put his finger on when it had started, but it was getting harder and harder to get your hands on appetizing food. Coffee shops were still open, the food franchises were operating too, but he was becoming increasingly aware of things running out. He hadn't had any of his favourite cereal for four weeks. So, once again, he settled for toast.

Still no reply from Carlos. It was fine, he'd do it on his own. But before he left the building, he needed to check out floor twenty-seven. At that time of day the lifts would be idle, so he could easily take a look to see if the rumours were true. Apparently there'd been some scene there. A child had been murdered by state police. He didn't believe it, but he wanted to see for himself.

As it turned out, the claims of a cordoned-off apartment were false. There was a sign on the door with the message *Home Sweet Home* attached to it and a tub filled with flowers to the side. It seemed that someone had recently moved in. In the corridor outside, the carpets had been newly scrubbed.

Alex got back into the lift and headed down to the ground floor. There were so many claims and rumours about, it was difficult to separate fact from fiction. Most of what he heard was rubbish, as far as he could tell.

Alex set off at a jog. So early in the morning he was able to make his way across the city swiftly. There was some traffic around, not too much, and barely any pedestrians.

As he neared City Park, he could hear chanting. A crowd had gathered to protest about something or other. This distraction might serve him well.

He checked the time. It was nearly half-past six. He couldn't have missed Jasmine Haworth – there were too many Troopers present, dressed in black and carrying guns.

'What's going on?' Alex asked a young couple as they walked towards him, ready to join the growing crowd.

'Don't you know?' the woman asked.

Alex shrugged.

'The authorities have kidnapped Professor Jasmine Haworth – you know, the professor from Sector 15, the one who's supposed to find a cure for the sickness. It's all over the darknet. Come and join us, somebody has got to stop Fortrillium!'

'Thanks, no, I'm fine. I was only wondering,' Alex replied, leaving them to walk on.

This was more of what Carlos and Deena had been saying. Conspiracy theories. And now, the darknet. They were correct in saying that Professor Haworth was arriving from City Airport. But she hadn't been kidnapped. It was an information swap with City22. His own mother had told him that much.

There was a stirring in the crowd. The Troopers were suddenly alert. A menacing green armored vehicle swept towards Fortrillium's main gate, followed by two black cars with mirrored windows, and then two more armored vehicles. Alex had never seen anything like it in the centre of the city.

In the grey early morning light, he saw a small flame – one, two, then more – and then, the crack of glass against metal. The front of the first armored vehicle was covered in flames, the paint beginning to blister as the heat intensified. More objects were hurled, more flames. There was a flurry of activity from the surrounding Troopers. The crowd was getting excited, the sight of fire and their panic emboldening them.

Out with Fortrillium!

Remember our constitutional rights!

Elected officials only – we're not a dictatorship!

Alex had heard it all before, albeit this type of thinking was becoming more common now.

Then, his mother stepped out of the first black car. She looked serious, in work mode, issuing commands through the Comms device on her breastplate. He'd not seen her new uniform yet. It was black and sturdy, she wore a breastplate and utility belt. She looked like a Trooper. He didn't like it. He'd never seen her look so threatening.

More bottles were thrown, and one landed right next to her. Yellow flames were licking her black suit. Two men in combat gear jumped out of the car, grabbed her and threw her to the ground, rolling her in the grass to stifle the fire.

The crowd surged forward. Shots rang out. The Troopers were firing on the crowd. Alex rushed towards the gunfire. He had to know his mum was safe. The protesters were screaming and hurling abuse, blocking the gate to the compound. He forced his way through the mob to where his mother was lying on the ground, dazed but safe, protected by her colleagues.

'Mum, are you okay?'

'Alex?'

She moved from professional mode to mum mode, then immediately back to being in charge.

'What on earth are you doing here? Get out! Go!'

Alex had to speak to Professor Haworth before she was inside the building. It might be his only chance. He wasn't going to listen. He couldn't let Audra down. She was somewhere inside that building and he was going to get her out.

Whatever had happened to her, Professor Jasmine Haworth was the key.

He vaulted onto the bonnet of the car and jumped down in front of Professor Haworth and her armed escort.

'My name is Alex Brady. Do you know Audra Woods?' he shouted at her. Two burley Troopers grabbed him and shoved him aside. He could hear Susan ordering them to leave him alone. Their hands moved to their weapons.

'Do you know Audra Woods?' he shouted again.

'Alex, for God's sake get out of here!'

His mum's cries could barely be heard over the sound of gunfire and screaming.

Jasmine Haworth looked up at him. She hesitated, as if she was about to speak, then one of her escorts pushed her forward.

'For God's sake, Alex, run, run for your life!'

Susan was on her feet, screaming at him, trying to battle her way through the chaos to get to her son.

As she was pushed through the heavy gates to Fortrillium, Professor Haworth turned to Alex. She spoke briefly to him before she disappeared inside the compound.

'She's our only hope now. We've got to do it ...'

The gates closed behind her. She was gone.

Alex heard a humming overhead. And the armed drones began to fire on the crowd below.

CHAPTER FOUR

'This is where you'll be spending your time from now on,' Kincade smiled, moving his hand to keep the double doors open.

Jasmine Haworth surveyed the area. Under any other circumstances she'd have been delighted. It was a purpose-built, state-of-the-art medical facility, better than she'd ever seen before. Everything they'd set out in the original specification was there. They'd been as good as their word on that.

'Where are my quarters? Am I confined to this building?'

Labatt answered this time. She'd already clocked that these men operated like some sinister double-act. She disliked both of them, which wasn't the best of starts to a new working relationship.

'Your accommodation is attached to this Med-Centre. You are forbidden to leave Fortrillium unless it's under armed escort and only then on pre-approved activities. You are Fortrillium's greatest asset, Professor Haworth.'

'And what about my husband? What about Magnus? Will you honour the terms of the agreement with City22?'

The two men looked at each other. She didn't need an answer in words, she'd just seen it for herself. From the moment she'd stepped off the plane at City Airport, the mood had changed. When that man – Richter – greeted her at the bottom of the steps with a small contingent of heavily armed troops, she could tell that this wasn't the exchange visit she'd been led to expect.

'All research breakthroughs will, of course, be shared with interested parties, with priority given to Sector 15,' Kincade said, ignoring her question.

Jasmine tried again.

'Why haven't I been taken directly to Magnus, as was agreed with President Lydon? That was a specific term of our agreement. Your President Henderson confirmed it in the Memorandum of Understanding.'

'Magnus is ... unwell,' Labatt answered. 'He's been working extremely hard to deliver this wonderful facility for you, and the poor man needs a rest. Don't worry, you will see him all in good time. Both of you are our guests here. We appreciate the gesture of goodwill from City22 in letting you come here. We are confident that your actions will help to assure the future of humanity.'

'Did we have any choice in the matter?'

Jasmine was aware that the men were losing patience.

'Professor Haworth, there is always a choice,' Kincade replied, looking at his watch. 'I'm going to leave you with Dr Labatt who will show you round. He will be your guide and mentor in the weeks ahead. Welcome, once again. I'd like to thank you on behalf of Fort ... on behalf of the President for joining us here.'

Kincade nodded to Labatt and left the Med-Centre. Jasmine moved towards the tech consoles to get a better look at the equipment. This was Magnus's work alright. He was a technical genius. Magnum Enterprises had brought untold benefits to the world in recent years. But now it seemed that, far from being changes for the better, they might be responsible for the downfall of the entire planet. A simple act of humanity, a leap into a potential new world – and now the survival of Earth itself was threatened. The medical professional in her relished the challenge. All she had ever wanted was to help her fellow men, and there could be no greater opportunity than now. But her excitement was tinged with doubt and worry.

At first, Magnus had been only too willing to travel to Sector 4. It was a short lecture circuit, sharing best practice and all the knowledge that his team had gathered to date. He was spurred by guilt, the concern that he and his organization were, in many ways, the architects of the current crisis. His impulse was for sharing and transparency. However, when the lecture tour ended and Magnus didn't return, alarm bells started to ring. When the World Health Organization confirmed that pandemic phase had been reached and the planet was at crisis point, she knew that he wasn't coming back.

According to Sector 4, his return was delayed because of problems with the paperwork. Everybody knew that it was now becoming extremely difficult to fly inter-state, while leaving the country was all but impossible unless you were military personnel or in government.

But when a delay of weeks turned to months and nobody in the Sector 15 state government was able to speak to Magnus, genuine concern set in. The situation began to resemble the negotiations for a hostage release.

At last Sector 4 struck a deal for his return. Contracts were signed for a voluntary information exchange between the two states. Magnus would be returned to Sector 15, while Jasmine would stay in Sector 4 for a period of no more than four weeks. It was rock solid legal, signed by two presidents, no less.

'I want to see Magnus as soon as possible. That was in the legal agreement. I refuse to begin work until I've seen him,' she told Labatt.

Jasmine suddenly noticed there were medical staff already at work in the facility. At first they'd appeared to be just running checks here and there, but Labatt clapped his hands and within seconds she realized she had become the patient rather than the doctor.

'Hop up on the couch, if you would. We need to give you the latest VaXX shots.'

A male nurse took her arm and began to guide her towards the couch.

'What is this? I have a right to know what you're injecting into me. Which VaXX shot is this? I'm already up-to-date.'

'Please, Professor Haworth, we have our own rules and regulations in this facility. It's vitally important that your shots are updated. You needn't worry, this was developed from research which your husband co-ordinated. Granted, we had to pull it up from the archives, but Magnus was happy to work with us on it. After a little encouragement.'

A second nurse took Jasmine's other arm and she was maneuvered onto the couch. Taken by surprise, she gave some small resistance, but still complied with the process.

'Every citizen in Sector 4 is getting this VaXX shot. It is now a legal requirement for our citizens. You'll note that the document to which you refer obliges you to recognize and abide by all state-wide legislative processes. This is one of them.'

Jasmine knew that she had to comply. If the VaXX shot

had been derived from Magnus's research it couldn't be all bad.

As a young man, Magnus had done some work for the military. She had no idea what it involved, but not long after came the First Global Crisis, which was caused by solar flares. Magnus hadn't been able to speak about any of it. A veil of secrecy had been drawn over the incident.

But from then on he'd vowed to ensure that his work would only be used to benefit humankind. And he'd been as good as his word. They'd seen incredible medical break-throughs in that time. Life expectancy had been increased dramatically. It was such a change from the world she'd been born into. And now ... it was all threatened by a simple oversight.

No, if Magnus was involved in the VaXX programme, it had to be about furthering humanity, not harming it. He'd sworn that much to her.

Before she knew it, she'd been given the VaXX shot. She'd administered thousands of injections in her time, but she still hated being on the receiving end of them. She'd urged Magnus to dedicate resources to finding an alternative, but in spite of the remarkable technological advancements all around them, delivery by needle remained the best way to immunize the masses. Labatt had not bothered to waste the new needle-free process on her. That was reserved for officials and politicians only.

'Excellent! We can now begin your induction.'

Dr Labatt moved forward and the medical staff dispersed as quickly as they'd gathered.

Jasmine rubbed her arm.

'Well done, Professor Haworth. You've had the latest VaXX shot ... plus a little something else to ensure that you remain completely focused on your work here. You now have the latest vaccine available. It's proved to be highly effective in delaying the next mutation of the virus. This will be shared through Global Consortium channels to satisfy the requirements of the worldwide medical framework.'

'What VaXX version are you on? Are you still on GPT23?'

'No. We've moved ahead of the rest of the world. Sector 4 has migrated to KLC2.3, and it's massively effective. We believe that we've made a major breakthrough. However, it's extremely expensive to produce and – frankly – it's going to split the world in two: those countries that can afford to produce it, and those that can't. In simple terms, we're going to have to start deciding who lives and who dies.'

Jasmine studied Labatt's face. She reckoned he was seventy or so, certainly late sixties. He was a sturdy man, his white beard neatly trimmed, and he had an authoritative air.

'We knew it might come to that,' she said slowly. 'It was always going to come down to expense and delivery.'

This was the scientist talking, the logical mind. But she and Magnus had fallen out about it.

'It's a numbers game, Magnus,' she'd tried to reason with him. 'It's impossible to protect everybody. It's too big a task. And if we try, we risk the whole system failing.'

Magnus was normally a calm man, but on this topic he became emotional. It was as if he'd seen this scenario before: some get to live, others get to die – it's just a numbers game, but the herd survives at all costs.

'These are human beings, not numbers,' he argued. 'For as long as I live I will maintain that there's always a techno-logical solution. Sometimes it just takes time.'

But Jasmine knew there wasn't much time left. To save lives, sometimes lives had to be lost. It was the dichotomy of her profession. Sometimes a mother has to die for a baby to survive. In other circumstances, the mother might live and the baby die. On a medical level, Labatt was making sense.

'Is that all you injected me with? You mentioned that Magnus's work had contributed in some way. Magnus is no doctor – nanotechnology is more his thing.'

'You've hit the nail right on the head!'

Labatt placed his hand on her back, as if he was about to give her a congratulatory pat.

'What is it? What did Magnus come up with?'

'It has nothing to do with the survival of the species, Professor Haworth. Quite the contrary, in fact. Your dear husband has helped us to revive a wonderful bit of technology that he created as a younger man, when he was contracted to the military. He thought he'd managed to bury it forever ... but let's just say, his idea has made a comeback. I'm delighted to say you're keeping it in the family by having it included in that VaXX shot. You're now the same as every other citizen in Sector 4. You have absolutely no cause for concern, if you remain fully compliant with the terms of the contract which was signed by your own president.'

'And if I don't? What happens then? What have you put in my body?'

'If you don't help us, Professor Haworth, you are putting the whole of humanity at risk. Sector 4 and its allies intend to survive at any cost. Let's just say we're beginning to introduce some elements of martial law in a backdoor manner.'

'You're kidding me? Our president has no knowledge of this. Martial law hasn't been sanctioned. What's going on?'

'The endgame is upon us, Professor Haworth. We have no intention of getting caught out while The Global Consortium debates what to do and ties us all up in red tape. We're in Phase 6 now, and when the time comes, we will be able to enforce martial law here with complete obedience.'

'And if we disobey? What happens then?'

'If any of our good citizens fail to see things the way we do – if they conspire to block the work we're doing to assure *their* survival? Well, in that situation, they give us no other choice. They'll be deleted.'

As she tumbled down the chute, Deena cursed her impetuousness, wondering what would be awaiting her at the bottom. Perhaps it would have been better to surrender to the Troopers after all.

There was plenty of room in the tube for her body, but her arms and elbows were clipped where the sections were connected, bruising and cutting her flesh. She tried to slow her descent by pushing her legs against the hard plastic sides, but if she slowed too much, Price or Scorsese might come crashing into her.

She braced herself for the impact. They were six floors up, the sort of distance where you'd probably die if you jumped. Was it possible to escape with no damage? She hoped so. Whatever happened, it would be better than a bullet. She could see the opening below her. The minute she landed, she would have to roll away to clear the exit for the next man down.

They were in luck. The skip was filled with screwed up balls of plastic sheeting and packaging materials from the appliances which had been installed six floors above them. As soon as she landed, Deena rolled to the side. Her whole body was sore but nothing was broken. Seconds behind her came Evan. Heavier than Deena, he landed hard and seemed stunned. His gun slipped out of his hand and became lost within the debris.

'Roll over, roll!' Deena shouted, but he was too slow.

It was only a matter of seconds before Scorsese appeared. Price had begun to move out of the way, but he'd taken too long about it, grasping to find his gun. Scorsese slammed against his left arm. Price screamed in agony.

'We need an ambulance!' Scorsese was panicking, the fabric of his jacket ripped to shreds showing the cut, raw flesh beneath

'We can't, they'll be back down here any minute, we have to run!' yelled Deena.

Price gasped, scarcely able to speak through the shock and pain.

'They're six floors up, they can be down in minutes. If we don't move, they'll catch us. That's your choice. A broken arm or a bullet.'

Encouraged by Deena's pleas, Price lowered himself over the side of the skip, cradling his damaged limb, beads of sweat standing out on his forehead. Scorsese put his arm round his waist to support him.

'We're at the back of the building,' Scorsese said. 'If we move fast, we'll be away before they get here.'

'Someone's following us down the chute. Help me move this plastic,' Deena cried.

They could hear the thudding and scraping sound of a body sliding downwards. Deena and Scorsese frantically pulled at the plastic to remove any chance of a soft landing. Troopers had body armor and helmets which would protect them on the way down through the sections of tubing. They were also armed.

Grimacing with pain, with his good arm Price threw a broken window frame over the side of the skip. Deena saw what he was doing and quickly moved it under the chute opening. There was a thump in the tube above their heads, and the Trooper slid out feet first, crashing into the window frame, bending the metal and smashing the remaining glass into jagged shards.

Deena watched in horror. It was a woman, not a man, and she was dying slowly, her suffering unimaginable. Perhaps she was a mother. Her gun fell out of the chute a few seconds later, nearly striking Deena on the head.

'Here, throw it over!' Price called.

Scorsese did as he was told. His face white and his hands shaking, he looked as if he was about to pass out from shock. Price rested the gun on the edge of the skip, levelled it at the Trooper and, with his good hand, squeezed the trigger.

'No!' shouted Deena, too late.

The Trooper's head dropped and she was still.

'They could have patched her up and saved her. You didn't need to do that!'

'There was no way she'd have survived those injuries. We had to put an end to her suffering. Come on, Deena. Snap out of it. We have to move.'

With a weapon in his good hand, Price had become the soldier he was meant to be. Scorsese helped Deena out of the skip and they sped along the alleyway which ran along the back of the apartment building.

'Where are we heading?' Scorsese panted. 'We need to get to a doctor. I have a friend round here, she'll help us.'

'We can't risk it. We need to find somewhere without cameras or surveillance,' said Price.

He was struggling to run in a way which didn't agitate his arm. He passed the gun to Scorsese.

'Is it broken?' Scorsese asked.

'Not broken, bruised and sprained,' Price replied. 'Give me your belt. If I can support it, that will help.'

'Follow my lead!' Deena urged, as Scorsese attended to Price's arm. Her tech was still in her bag, making it hard for her too to move at speed. 'I know a place we can lie low for a while, where we can figure out what to do next.'

They stuck to the back streets. On the main roads they could hear sirens wailing and the screech of tires. It was clear they'd jumped right into an anthill.

They approached an open space between two apart-ment blocks. It was cordoned off with builders' fencing panels.

'It's along here,' Deena said.

She squeezed through a gap in the fence and the others followed.

'What is this place?' Scorsese asked.

'You'll find out soon enough. It's one of the reasons I was coming to see you this evening. At least now you'll believe me when I show you.'

There was sufficient light to find their way around the site. Sections of huge concrete pipes were stacked to one side. They guessed it must be a sewerage project.

Deena stepped up to a digger, which had been parked next to the fence. She ran her hand along the rim of the tyre and held up a metal key. A couple of metres away was a brand new manhole cover which had clearly been recently cemented into place.

'Some things never change,' she smiled, inserting the

key into the metal disc. 'We'll be safe down here until things die down a bit. The Troopers will be crawling all over this area tonight. It's clean – there's no water, it hasn't been put into use yet.'

'How do you know about this place?' Scorsese asked, looking down the hole into the dark below. 'This is a building site. No one's allowed on it without permission.'

'Ever the public servant, Mr Scorsese,' Deena replied. 'But this is much more than a building site. My friend Audra and I discovered something mind-blowing down here, and I'm convinced it's the reason she has disappeared. No one's seen her for over a year now. Sure, I know it looks like they're just building a sewer, but this is Fortrillium's work. Whatever they're building in these pipes has nothing to do with the city's sewerage system.'

As Alex turned to make his escape, he saw his mother fall to the ground. A bullet fired from one of the drones had grazed her right arm.

'Mum!' he screamed.

It was mayhem. The protesters were panicking, scattering in all directions, desperate to get away. Someone shouted at him to run. Alex looked behind him. Susan was moving, she was talking. One of her colleagues was taking care of her.

Why couldn't his mother be a teacher or a lawyer? When he was younger, he'd been so proud of her job, but now, with the creeping tentacles of Fortrillium spreading throughout Sector 4, it had become a problem.

He'd been a fool to come to this place, but it had been his only chance to speak to Professor Haworth. She'd confirmed that the message from Audra was genuine. 'She's our only hope now,' Jasmine Haworth had told him, before the iron gates of Fortrillium closed behind her.

The bullets fired over the crowd, ricocheting from pavements and walls. The drones swept along the street, stalking their prey. The Troopers were spreading out and detaining those people who hadn't been shot. The drones issued warnings with monotone, synthesized voices.

Stop! You are guilty of a public order offence. Surrender to a State Trooper or you will be shot! This will be your only warning.

Alex had heard stories of this type of behaviour before, but he hadn't believed them. The internet was heavily regulated, very little came through which wasn't Fortrillium or public information oriented, so he'd dismissed it as crazy rumours.

More shots, more screams. The protesters were being rounded up. Troopers were approaching from the top of the street. Soon he'd have nowhere to run. Suddenly he was aware of someone next to him, someone who had locked onto him while he was running.

'Alex, duck in here. We can hide in the park.'

'Carlos! I thought you weren't coming. Where were you? Did you see what happened?'

'It's happening, man. This is what I warned you about. It's happening all over the state. You'll never hear about it on the News Feed, but it's the end of the world. I'm telling you.'

Carlos steered Alex through a gap in the fence. The work to claim the last part of City Park for Fortrillium had already started, but it was still possible to find trees and shrubs to provide cover. As Alex squeezed through the fence into the shadows of the park, he saw a Trooper pointing at him from way up the street.

'Carlos, we've got to hurry. We've been spotted. I know where we are – we can hide by Audra's tree. I want to show you something.'

They were in the undergrowth now, not far from the bridge next to the tree where Audra's Memory Tab was placed.

They could hear voices a couple of hundred metres behind them.

'They've followed us! Come on, after me, Carlos. We need to climb down the bank to get there. They won't see us – they'll head over the bridge.'

They dodged into the bushes and made their way towards the tree where Alex and Audra had spent so much time talking.

'The Memory Tab ... it's gone!'

'What?'

'I had a Memory Tab here – for Audra. It's been removed.'

'Keep your voice down, man. They're getting closer.'

Alex continued in a whisper.

'You're going to think I'm going crazy. Am I losing it? I feel like I don't know what's real and what's imaginary any longer. But I came here only yesterday, and I swear there was a message from Audra on the Memory Tab. She told me to speak to Professor Haworth, and that's why I came here this morning. Audra's alive, Carlos. And she's in danger. She looked terrified. We have to find her. She's in that building. I know it!'

Carlos looked at his friend, and then towards the bridge where one of the Troopers was standing, scanning the area.

'Where's the other one?' Carlos asked, looked around.

'They've got weapons, man. Stay quiet. These guys mean business.'

There was the crack of a breaking twig. About twenty metres away, the second Trooper was making his way through the trees behind them. He must have given some kind of signal, as the Trooper on the bridge started to walk towards them.

Alex started, realizing what was happening. They knew where they were hiding. Could they see them by the tree?

'Wait, don't move,' Carlos said, in a voice that was barely audible. Alex noticed that in the distance the shooting had stopped. The protesters must have been rounded up.

'You should go, Carlos. It's me they want. You weren't a protester, you were just passing by. Make a run for it. I'll give myself up.'

Carlos looked at him and nodded. He moved to the side, away from the path of the approaching Troopers. Alex stood up.

'I'm over here!' he called out, looking to make sure that Carlos had got away. 'I give myself up. I'm over here!'

The footsteps were getting closer and closer, crackling through the undergrowth. Within seconds, they were in front of him, weapons trained directly at his head. One woman and one man.

'What do you reckon?' the woman asked.

'Not sure I can be bothered with the paperwork. It's been a long shift. Shall we?'

'They'll be leveling this part of the park in the next few days. Have you seen the size of those trucks? I bet nobody will notice.'

'You think Kincade even cares? You heard what he said:

We're either with him and we flourish – or we're his enemy and we perish. I want to live, and I'm betting you do too?'

They were going to shoot him. Alex closed his eyes. How had it come to this?

He heard a thud, then a gasp. He opened his eyes, just in time to see a helmet roll up to his feet. He looked up as the headless body of the male Trooper crumpled to the ground. To his right, the female Trooper was on her knees, a knife plunged into her heart.

From the shadow of Audra's tree, Carlos emerged, the blade of his katana stained with blood. Before Alex could stop him, he had removed the second Trooper's head. As she hit the ground, he retrieved his wakizashi and wiped it on her trousers.

'They were going to kill you,' he said. 'And I don't leave my friends to fend for themselves. Ever.'

CHAPTER FIVE

'I want to see my husband!'

Jasmine Haworth was about to step on a hornet's nest and she could see the insects getting their stings ready for her.

'You have what you want. I'm here. I can't go anywhere – you have me trapped. So I want to see Magnus.'

Labatt smiled at her. He seemed to be relishing her discomfort. He was enjoying this induction, it fed the part of him that was devoid of humanity.

'All in good time, Professor Haworth. First, you will be taken on a tour of the facility and find out how things work here. I have to inform you that the agreement between our two states is worthless and we do not intend to honour it. You should understand that from the outset. You are now on Fortrillium property, and if your amateur legal teams had done their homework properly, they'd have seen that the area of land that was once called City Park has been reclassified. It is within Sector 4 but no longer bound by its legislation. Under the new constitution, it makes its own rules.'

'You're insane!'

This was the stuff of nightmares. From Command HQ in Sector 15 they'd had no idea this was going on.

'When the inevitable comes, Professor Haworth, Sector 4 will be one of the last states standing. Cities 22, 27, 37, 60 – they're all as good as dead already. Too little, too late. Have no doubt about it, when the final mutation begins, we will be ready for it. And you will be a part of that. You and your husband.'

'This is crazy. The whole point of The Global Consortium is to prevent a catastrophe like this. We're all in this together. If one of us can survive, we can all survive.'

'It's not quite like that though, is it, Professor Haworth? You haven't been entirely honest with The Consortium yourself. You know what's coming ... why do you think you're our guest at the moment?'

Jasmine blushed scarlet. She felt as if she was burning up. She could only repeat: 'I want to see my husband. I don't start work until I know he's safe.'

While they'd been talking, a young man with an air of earnestness about him had entered the room. He was dressed in a suit and wore a tie. He had the look of somebody who was sure of his position. He was now standing beside them.

'This is James Morgan. He will show you around. I look forward to working with you, Professor Haworth. Whatever our differences in approach, ultimately we're after the same thing.'

He walked off, leaving Jasmine with Morgan.

'What are you, some kind of civil servant?' she asked, much more rude and dismissive than she would be under normal circumstances.

She was exhausted. She'd been working twenty-hour days in Sector 15. The clock was ticking. Phase 6 was upon them. The endgame. She reckoned they had six months at most until the final mutation. Labatt was right about that: Sectors 15, 13, 3 – they were behaving as though they were searching for a cure to the common cold, as if they had all the time in the world.

'You could call me a civil servant,' Morgan replied. 'But I prefer to think of myself as the future President of Sector 4.'

She was taken aback by the sheer egotism of the man.

'You're kidding, right?'

She waited for his mouth to upturn into a grin. It didn't.

'We live in exceptional times, Professor Haworth. I may be young, but Fortrillium is the future of our state and a president who works with the organization, rather than fighting it, will be much more productive for the population. I will be that president. In difficult times, different people get to thrive. I intend to be one of them.'

It seemed remarkable to Jasmine that a man so young could even contemplate such a career trajectory. At his age she was still studying psychology, the academic discipline which allowed her to identify this man as a narcissist. When she first met Magnus, she'd feared that he too possessed that personality trait. But time had taught her she was mistaken. Her husband was powerful and knowledgeable, but far from being self-regarding, he used his talents to look outwards and benefit humanity. Her gut told her that Morgan was the real thing.

'Follow me please, Professor Haworth. Your first shift begins in just under one hour. Daily shifts within the research facility run from 07:00 hours until 22:00 hours, and you will be expected to begin work immediately.'

'You must be joking. I've been on a plane, subjected to your ridiculous border controls, and had to be escorted through a mob. You're really expecting me to start work immediately?'

Morgan ignored her and walked out of the medical facility. Fortrillium was vast. In happier times, Jasmine had walked in City Park and enjoyed its beauty. She'd first visited the city as a child, taken by her parents. Recalling those carefree times felt like breathing purified air, it was exhilarating. She'd been in and out of the city as an adult, usually attending conferences, and she'd always made time to visit the park.

She was astonished to see what had happened to the vast open space. It was as if Fortrillium's dark establishment had always occupied that spot. Any greenery was fast being obliterated. And now, here she was, seeing exactly what had replaced it.

She followed Morgan as he strode confidently through long corridors, passing doors marked as Hazardous Area or Authorized Personnel Only.

'What does President Henderson make of all this?' she asked, a little breathless at the speed they were walking.

'I don't know how the constitutional changes are working in Sector 15, but here the President is little more than a figurehead. Sure, the legal power still resides with him, but in reality? In reality, Fortrillium is in charge of Sector 4, or at least it soon will be. My advice to you would be to embrace it. You don't have any children, do you? I read the briefings. It's only you and your husband. You have nothing to lose, nobody else to worry about. My advice would be to fully engage in what's going on. You have the best facilities and massively increased chances of survival. There's a chance to make history. Not at some insignificant level either. What we're doing here is essential.'

That might indeed be the case, but it was the methodology that Jasmine doubted. A woman's screams were coming from one of the rooms to her left. The screams were of pain – excruciating, persistent pain.

'What's going on in there? What are you doing in this place?'

Morgan considered his answer. He didn't flinch as the cries filled the concrete anonymity of the corridor.

'Political prisoners,' he said coldly. 'You must have them in Sector 15. Sabotage and conspiracy. You of all people know that it has to be stamped on. We have to focus on the central problem. These people are a distraction.'

'You're not ... you're not torturing them, are you?'

Jasmine took his arm, forcing him to stop walking and face her.

'Interrogating,' he replied. 'It's a completely different thing. If you thought your system of government was at risk of being undermined, wouldn't you do the same? You know the protocols, Professor Haworth. The government must rule for the good of the people. With no government to coordinate things, particularly at times like these, we're already dead.'

He continued walking. Jasmine hovered at the door for a moment. It had an electronic lock. The howls emanating from the room seemed like the accusatory cries of her conscience. Dare she refuse to work? What would happen if she did? Might she – or Magnus – end up incarcerated?

She wasn't certain if she had the courage to fight them. Morgan's summary of her position had been astute. She would have better facilities in this place than they'd given her in Sector 15. That had felt more like a makeshift military medical facility than a BioLab. He was right. They were deluded if they thought they had time to spare. The horror was coming to wipe them all out – they were barely keeping ahead with the VaXX programmes. Already The Global Consortium was denying access to the latest vaccines, marking out the countries they would abandon first, those with the fewest resources. It was like letting your weakest children die so they wouldn't take the food of the strongest.

From the BioLab, Morgan took her along a series of corridors leading to what seemed to be a dedicated underground rail service. Jasmine was astonished at what they'd achieved in a small amount of time. Is this what it took to survive? This ruthless determination?

There was a train standing at the platform. They got on board and Morgan placed his hand on a pad inside the carriage. The sliding doors closed silently and the shuttle began to move, immediately picking up speed. There were no engine sounds to be heard, only the flash of lights within the darkness of the tunnel to indicate that they were moving. In less than a minute they had arrived at their destination: a vast underground security facility.

From the moment she stepped off the shuttle, it was clear to Jasmine that this was an underground prison. It was heavily guarded and fortified, and the cold iron bars, the armed security guards and the prevalence of security cameras sent a chill through her.

They walked through a dimly lit corridor to emerge in a vast chamber lined with cages. They were filled with men, women and even some children. Morgan was well known. He clearly had the run of the place. Maybe he *would* be President one day, Jasmine thought. In the centre of the domed area was a tower circled by armed guards watching the activity in the cages. The voices and cries of those imprisoned there echoed in the hollowness of the cavern. There was a rush of cool air which suggested immediately that there were no luxuries here, no heating. The stench was immediate and intense, Jasmine struggled to maintain her composure. Like dogs in a pound, there was a spark of excitement among the inmates at this unexpected presence in the prison.

'My God, what is this place?' she asked. It seemed to her to be the beginnings of hell, but the devil had only just got started.

'This is where you will extract your live test subjects. While you work on Fortrillium property, there are no human rights obligations. You may run large-scale simulations in contained areas without any fear of legal restitution at a later date. In short, Professor Haworth, you should feel free to kill as many of these prisoners as you wish to achieve a vaccine for the plague. Because if you don't find a vaccine, they're all dead anyway.'

It was pitch black in the sewer pipes. Deena was thankful that they were dry and unused. It might not be such a great place to hide once the city's waste began to flow through them.

'Who has their phone?' she asked.

There was a shuffling next to her and Scorsese's face appeared, lit up by the torch on his device.

'This is about all it's good for these days,' he said, moving it away from his face and shining it ahead. 'Wretched things are not much use as phones now.'

He was right about that. Most people carried them out of habit rather than utility. Out-of-state phone mast access had been blocked when the state borders were closed. It had

'I'm trying, I'm trying! I've moved the first bolt, but the second is sticking!'

Distance one metre. You are unauthorized personnel. One minute to impact. This is your final opportunity to evacuate before termination.

Scorsese was now looking directly into the blade of the machine.

'I can't believe it!' Deena screamed. 'The key just broke off in my hand. We're stuck.'

'Alex, you have to pull yourself together.'

Carlos spoke in a calm and measured voice. He'd never removed a human head before. He wasn't a killer by nature, but he understood when violence was the only option.

He'd been warning Alex for months, but his friend was in denial. How much more would Fortrillium have to take away before people finally realized what was going on?

'I can't believe you did that.'

'Alex, they were about to shoot you.'

'But you cut their heads off.'

'They were going to kill you so they could get home on time, Alex. You were going to save them some paperwork. That's how concerned they were about you.'

Alex looked at the two headless bodies slumped in front of him on the ground. He couldn't take it in. It had happened so fast.

Carlos picked up one of the helmets and shook it so that the head fell onto the ground. Alex turned away and vomited into a bush behind him. Carlos was trying his best to be strong, but even he felt as if his legs would give way beneath him.

'We have to see this through,' he said, keeping his voice as steady as possible. 'If you want to see Audra, we have to get into that building. And now is the time to do it.'

Alex knew he was right, but that didn't stop him wanting to scream out loud. This was the turning point. He'd dreamed about Audra, he'd always felt she was alive. And now he had proof. She'd sent him the video, and Professor Haworth had all but confirmed it. It was time for him to take responsibility. He had a choice: to run away or to enter Fortrillium. He chose Audra.

Carlos handed him the helmet and turned to shake the head out of the second one. He was astonished at the clean cut made by his blade. He'd always assumed that it would be nothing like practising with cabbages. As it turned out, it was exactly like cabbages.

'We need to get these uniforms on. Take all the kit and the weapons. We're going in.'

Alex knew he was right. They undressed the dead Troopers, rolling their torsos and severed heads into the lake. Their resting place would be the foundations of Fortrillium. He wondered if these people had families to return to. What had made them turn so violently against fellow citizens – people they might have shared a seat with on the bus, or a sofa in a coffee shop? He'd been too slow to catch on. Carlos and Deena were way ahead of him.

'Are you bringing the big sword?' Alex asked.

'No, I can't conceal the katana in this uniform. I'll take the wakizashi instead. It's half the size and easier to hide. Ever used a gun before?'

'What do you think?' Alex picked up one of the guns and gave it the once-over. 'Have you?'

'I've done some target shooting on our farmland. Just cabbages. Until today, I've only ever killed vegetables.'

Alex chuckled. It seemed crazy to be laughing after what had happened, but it served as a welcome release of tension.

'Come on, let's join up with the other Troopers.'

Alex put on the helmet. It was heavy and cumbersome. And it was still warm.

They headed back out of the park and onto the road. There were bodies everywhere, lying in pools of blood. Ahead was a cluster of Troopers guarding those protesters who hadn't run fast enough to get away. Alex and Carlos joined them and simply followed the lead of the others. No questions were asked, no ID was required.

'Isn't that Harley over there?' Carlos whispered as they began to herd the crowd towards the entrance of Fortrillium.

'Yes, that's him. Fortrillium Youth Wing's star pupil. Look at him brandishing that gun. He loves it, it's what every bully dreams of.'

It wasn't long before they reached the main gates. The black cars had gone and the bodies were being removed; the drones had returned to wherever it was they had come from. Soon there would be no indication of what had happened here. The deception would continue.

The prisoners walked through the heavy compound gates to where a new group of Troopers were waiting to receive them. As the gates began to close again, a man and a woman broke free of the group and ran towards the outside. There was a ripple of excitement. Then two shots. The man dropped to the ground first, then the woman, both shot cleanly through the head. Across the courtyard, Harley stood grinning, his weapon perfectly steady, his arm still outstretched. The bodies were pulled safely within the compound and the gates locked. There were congratulations all round for Harley.

Everyone who entered the main building had to pass through one of two body scanners. Carlos and Alex hung back. Would they be found out? Harley pushed his way into the queue directly in front of them.

'Excuse me, gents. You don't mind if I go ahead of you?'

Carlos shook his head, not wanting to speak. Harley would recognize their voices immediately if he heard them, and he'd have no qualms about ratting them out.

Before long it was Harley's turn to go through security. He stepped forward, cocky and familiar with the personnel who were running the checks. The scanner to his side became free, and Alex and Carlos moved over to the other gate.

Alex went first. He held his breath as he passed through the machine. The last time he'd seen something like that was at the airport when he'd been going on holiday with his mum and dad. He remembered how happy he'd been, how carefree. It seemed like a different life.

He passed through, no challenges. He was in.

Carlos moved into the scanner at the same time as Harley. He could hear him sharing details of the courtyard incident with the security guard.

As Alex stood waiting for his friend, he could feel his energy fading. The sudden calm hit him like a wave. He wanted to close his eyes and sleep. And when he woke up, he wanted it to be in a world with Audra, his father out of prison, and his mum still working on the force. What he'd seen that day had made him realize that was never going to happen. Not unless he took action to change things.

His sense of inner peace was interrupted by the sound of a piercing electronic alert. Security staff were suddenly tense, weapons ready and pointing at the scanners. Both Carlos and Harley were standing with their arms in the air, the scanning devices circling around them, a blue light flashing. Two members of the security team moved in to investigate.

'Stay still, hands in the air!' one shouted.

They'd almost made it into Fortrillium, he was so close to Audra, Alex could feel it. It had to be the wakizashi that had set off the alarms. Everything else had passed directly through the scanners. Alex prepared himself for the inevitable. The game was up.

CHAPTER SIX

'May I speak to the prisoners?' Jasmine asked. 'I'd like to meet some of them, get a feel for what I'm working with here.'

'Be my guest,' Morgan replied. 'But take my advice, don't get too close. They smell. We spray them off properly before we start working with them. You'll soon get used to it. They're scum, this lot.'

He waved over two of the guards.

'I'd like you to see the Immune before the end of the day. She's quite something. That's where we need to focus your efforts. I'll make sure she's ready for you. Get an escort to C-Wing when you're done here.'

He headed back to the shuttle, leaving her in the care of the guards. Jasmine looked at them, but their faces were hidden by their helmets. It was nothing like this in City22, but then she knew their President had no conception of the gravity of the crisis facing humanity. Perhaps this was the only way.

'I'd like to speak to the prisoners alone.'

'That's not happening, Professor Haworth,' said the Trooper closest to her. 'You may talk to them through the bars, but there must be an armed guard in attendance at all times. I can stand out of earshot if the conversation refers to the project, but you're not permitted inside the cells or to speak to inmates who aren't cuffed.'

'What I want to talk about does relate to the project. It's confidential.'

'No problem.'

The guard looked up at the tower and spoke into his radio. Jasmine saw guns being moved, pointing towards where she was standing.

'If there's any trouble, stand aside,' he said. 'We'll take care of it.'

Jasmine nodded. She paused for a moment to survey the cages. The place was vast; it looked like it was capable of housing thousands of inmates, all deep underground with no natural light. It was a living grave.

She estimated it must measure at least 100 metres from the ground to the domed roof. Layers of platforms were built one above the other around three sides of the structure and on these the metal cages were placed. It was capable of housing many more prisoners in the future.

The smell was terrible. She recoiled as she approached the bars of the nearest cage.

'Keep your distance. No crossing the line!' the guard shouted.

She assumed it was in case anybody grabbed her. In front of her were skeletal men like scarecrows, their long beards matted, holding out their hands, imploring her to help them. It was impossible to tell how old the women were. Their clothes were rags, their hair lank and greasy, and in their eyes a look of desperation. In the corner of each cage was a bucket they used as a toilet. Jasmine wanted to scream.

'Can you get a message out to my wife ...'

'Help us, please help us ...'

'They torture us, you have to get us out of this place ...'

The voices might as well have been her conscience taunting her to do what she knew was right.

One voice stood out. It was the name that caught her attention.

'I need to get a message to my wife and my son – Susan and Alex Brady. Can you help?'

'Who said Alex Brady? Who was that?'

A man stepped forward.

'It was me. I'm Michael Brady, my son is Alex, my wife is Susan. Do you know them?'

'Perhaps,' she replied, looking at the man. He was a mess, yet his voice was confident, educated. This man didn't seem to be a common criminal.

'Why are you here?' Jasmine asked.

'Why is anybody here?' There was anger in his voice. 'You have to get the message out. The world has to know what's going on. They're killing people. I was being held in a proper prison awaiting trial when I was brought here. This is barbaric. We have human rights!'

There were two shots from the tower. It seemed they were fired as a warning.

'Keep the noise down!' the guard shouted, as much to Jasmine as to the prisoners.

'Have you seen a man called Magnus here? You might have seen him on your flat screens before you were imprisoned here. He's tall with grey hair and a beard, about sixty. He's my husband. I'm looking for him.'

'No, I've never heard of him,' Michael answered.

Jasmine looked back at the guard to make sure he wasn't listening.

'What are they doing to you here?'

'Don't tell me you don't know!'

'I've just arrived, from City22. It's different there. I came here to help ... to find Magnus ... this is new to me. I'm as horrified as you are.'

'They're using us for live experiments. They take us ten at a time, at random. Nobody ever comes back. Men, women, kids – it doesn't matter.'

There were three more shots, and this time a woman in the next cage was hit by a bullet. The inmates around her shrank back, watching as she bled out in front of them.

'That's enough,' said the guard. 'Professor Haworth, come with me.'

'Remember: Susan and Alex Brady. Let them know I'm here. At least let them know I'm alive.'

Jasmine nodded. She was trying to recall the name of the youth who'd accosted her in the crowd earlier. At the time she'd been frightened. She wasn't really listening. But now she thought about it, she was certain he'd said Alex Brady.

'Doctor Labatt is ready for you.'

The guard indicated that she should follow him.

As they arrived at C-Wing, Jasmine was deep in thought. The part of her that was medical expert had been waiting for this. She was about to meet the one person who might be able to save them all. Professionally, this is what she lived for, but she wondered if the price would be too high.

The guard stopped in front of a windowless white door with a sign in large red letters: *Strictly Authorized Personnel*

Only. He held a key card against an electronic control panel, it recognized his security clearance and the heavy door slid open silently.

A young woman was secured upright in front of them, strapped to a rectangular metal operating table. Small strips of skin had been taken from her arms and legs, as if she was being slowly skinned alive. Tubes ran in and out of her body, wiring her into a bank of terminals monitoring every aspect of her biology. Her eyes flickered as the door closed behind Jasmine, but they didn't open. She grimaced, as if expecting some new sample to be taken or another needle to pierce her skin. Jasmine had never seen anything as shocking in her life. She felt a wave of nausea pass over her. She thought she was going to faint.

'Takes some getting used to, but it's necessary, I'm afraid.'

Labatt spoke calmly, as if he'd grown accustomed to these atrocities some time ago.

'Professor Haworth, meet our single best hope of survival. This is Audra Woods, the world's first known Immune.'

The machine was so close to them that Deena could feel the air from the blades blowing across her face. She looked up at it and then back towards Scorsese.

'Run! Go back as far down the tunnel as you can!'

'But there's no way out down there. We're cornered. We're going to be shredded.'

'Trust me! And throw that gun over here, Evan.'

Scorsese looked uncertain, but they were out of options.

He had no idea how to get them out of there, so if Deena had a plan – however crazy – it would be their best chance. Evan threw the gun over to him and he passed it up to Deena.

'Now run!' she shouted.

Scorsese did as he was told. Deena pushed the weapon inside the waistband of her trousers, then stretched out her arms towards the jammed manhole cover. The tip of the macerator's frame touched her foot as she pulled herself up to the roof of the tunnel. Below the cover was a circular space. Deena had worked out that there was enough room for her to pull herself above the bladed unit if she rested her back against one side of the concrete entrance and pushed her feet against the other. It took all her strength to keep herself suspended above the blades.

Slowly the machine was inching beneath her. The grinding and clanking of the metal on concrete was deafening. Deena gritted her teeth. Every joint, every sinew was on fire, her spine racked with the pain of being compressed in such a tight space. Her heart was thudding in her chest. Her grip was loosening, she was slipping down. She couldn't hold on any longer. She dropped to the ground, just behind the machine.

Then, something she hadn't expected. The macerator stopped dead in its tracks, the blades still turning. The presence of a new intruder behind it seemed to have confused its sensors.

Multiple intruders detected. Imminent danger of termination. This is your final warning. Evacuate the area immediately.

Deena froze. Would it turn back and try to eliminate her first? She could see Scorsese and Evan ahead through the spinning blades. They were panicking, shouting at each other.

The machine began to move once more. For an instant it lurched towards Deena before continuing its journey towards the two men ahead of it. Standing directly behind the deadly device, she examined its frame for a control panel. She'd bought them a little more time, but she knew that the sewer pipes were a work in progress and would be sealed off at the end. Scorsese and Evan would be trapped.

She could hear Scorsese's frantic cries over the noise of the machine. She looked beyond him to see a second macerator at the end of the pipe. He and Price were boxed in. There was no escape. Closer and closer the machines moved towards the frightened men. Electronic messages warned them of their impending termination.

Unauthorized personnel. This is a secure area. Under section 46.7v2 of the Fortrillium Sector 4 Security Directive, termination is now sanctioned by law.

Deena estimated she had no more than three minutes until the men were sandwiched between the blades of the two macerators. She had to stay calm. She shone her phone light around the frame. It was only a machine. There had to be a way of disabling it.

Then she saw it. A small black metal flap. In the darkness it was easy to miss. As she reached out to open it and uncover the panel within, a powerful electrical shock threw her to the floor. It must have been activated as a deterrent.

'Damn it!'

She picked herself up and ran back to the macerator. She removed her jacket and wrapped it around her right hand. She knew she needed insulation. She shone the light from her phone towards the open panel. There was an emergency switch, but it seemed to be key operated.

Scorsese and Evan's cries were becoming increasingly desperate.

'Deena, come on!'

'For God's sake, turn the thing off!'

She tried to shut out their voices and focus on the problem. If she lost her cool, it would all be over. She reckoned they had a minute, maybe even less now. And once the machines had sliced the two men, they would come for her. Who knew how many of the things were down in these tunnels?

Deena thought fast. The macerators appeared to be electrical, not engine driven, and that meant they could be discharged or shorted. Yes, the device had given her an electric shock, but it hadn't been powerful enough to kill her. She had to cut off its power supply. She looked up. Evan was so close now that they could have reached out and touched hands if the blades hadn't been turning. She was out of choices.

She unwrapped the jacket from her hand and let it drop to the ground. It wasn't insulation she needed. Deena realized she'd have to take the full charge in her own body — either to short it or drain its power. The machines were now so close to Scorsese and Evan that they had to stand side by side to stay clear of the deadly blades. If her plan didn't work, at least she'd be out cold by the time the machines came back for her.

She lurched towards the electrical panel, placing one hand on the protective flap and the other on the outer rim of the macerator. She was expecting the kick this time and it came. A strong electrical jolt shot through her body. She felt as if she was being shaken by a massive hand, which was trying to throw her off the machine. With every last bit of willpower that she could summon, Deena hung on to the device, absorbing the shocks. She knew she mustn't let go.

She was dazed, sweating, and weakening by the second. Her body convulsed, her heart struggling to maintain its regular beat. Scorsese and Evan were now close enough to whisper to. She heard some electrical sparking. The sounds had changed. She couldn't take it anymore, she had to release her grip. She collapsed onto the cold concrete base of the sewer pipe.

Minutes later, she woke to see a face above her. Two faces. The light was poor, they were somewhere dark. She was dazed and confused.

'We thought we'd lost you there,' Evan said. 'That was some rescue, Deena. How are you feeling?'

It came back to her. The tunnel. The machines. Scorsese and Evan. If they'd told her she'd been hit by a truck, she wouldn't have been surprised.

'What happened?'

She was trying to organize her thoughts.

'You blew the machine,' Scorsese said. He held out his arm. 'Look, it was so close the blade sliced off a bit of my sleeve. I thought we were goners, I really did. I don't know how to thank you.'

'I had the job of bringing you back from the dead,' Evan smiled. 'Well, Scorsese had to do the work, my arm wasn't up to it. But I talked him through it. I've only had to do that once before, with a fellow soldier. It's part of the training. Your ribs will be sore — sorry about that. But there was no way you were dying on me after getting us out of that scrape. No way!'

'What about the second machine?'

'The moment you stopped the first one, the blades stopped dead. I'll bet my life it's sent out some kind of alert.

If what you say about that wiring is true, they won't want any snoopers down here,' said Scorsese.

'We have to move,' Evan said. 'And fast. If they do know there are intruders down here, it won't take them long to figure out who it is. Can you move yet, Deena?'

'I'll need a minute or two.'

'Let me have that broken key,' Scorsese said. 'Let's see if I can get the cover off now we've bought ourselves some time.'

Deena handed it to him. It was only the top that was broken. There was enough of it to use, but there simply hadn't been time to fiddle with it with the machine coming after them.

As she lay on the ground, she could hear Evan and Scorsese further along the corridor. They were figuring out how to get the manhole cover open with the damaged key. Then, success. She detected it in the tone of their voices. She had to rally herself; that was all the recovery time she was getting. She staggered to her feet. She bent down to pick up her jacket and slowly put it on. Her body ached, she was cold now, but her mind was steadying and she was able to follow what was going on around her.

Scorsese was next to her.

'We've unlocked it. We need to get out of here. I'll carry your bag.'

Deena was standing directly below the manhole cover.

'I thought you'd opened it,' she said.

'We have,' said Evan. 'It's unlocked. You need to push it up. We didn't want to risk leaving it open.'

'I don't think my legs will hold steady enough. Can you help me up?'

Scorsese knelt down and cupped his hands, ready for Deena's boot. She stepped up, reaching out her arms to slide away the cover above her. Scorsese pushed her upwards. As her head emerged into the fresh air, she grabbed the sides of the circular entrance and hoisted herself out onto the ground.

While she lay on her front, trying to catch her breath, she became aware that she wasn't alone.

'Put your hands behind your head and stay completely still. This is Fortrillium property and you are trespassing. I'm going to need to check your ID.'

Carlos lowered his raised hands and stepped forward, away from the scanner. The blue light was still flashing. Alex held his breath. This was it. They'd been found out. First his friend would be searched and apprehended, and then they would come for him. But, as he watched, he saw Carlos walk confidently away.

Meanwhile, Harley was surrounded by armed security personnel and forced to the ground, his hands behind his head.

'I switched it!' Carlos whispered. 'Come on ... before he realizes what's going on.'

Behind them, Alex caught sight of the wakizashi as it was taken from Harley's body armor. Harley would know who that belonged to. It wouldn't take them long to figure out what had happened.

'How did you do that? I was standing right by you and I didn't see that going on.'

'When you learn to handle one of those things correctly, you pick up other tricks along the way. It's all about focus, mind and dexterity. And that idiot Harley was so busy mouthing off that he made it easy. He thought I was patting him on the back to congratulate him. We're inside Fortrillium, Alex. I can't believe it!'

'I wish I could speak to Mum. She was hurt, I'm worried about her.'

'Susan will be fine,' Carlos reassured him. 'You saw her talking – she isn't badly hurt, just her arm. And you need to trust her, Alex. She's a highly trained cop, the best in her field.'

Alex wasn't so sure. Things were getting out of control. The path ahead was filled with hazards, and he was terrified by the brutality that he'd seen that day. It was why Fortrillium had succeeded in grabbing so much power and so soon. Each little bite could be brushed aside ... but soon the irritation became a festering wound that needed to be lanced.

They walked rapidly along the grey, featureless corridor.

'This place is huge!' Carlos said. 'And once they colonize the remainder of City Park, it'll be even bigger.'

Alex waited for two women in white coats to pass by before he spoke.

'Why do they need something this size?'

'Officially, it's for governance. But you're right. There's much more going on behind the scenes.'

'I can't believe it. It wasn't that long ago that no one had heard of Fortrillium, and we were going about our everyday lives.'

'If you ask me, it's a power grab. They're creating a police state. The President has little or no control over what's happening. In theory, the constitutional power is his, but you've seen what they're like. Do you still think Fortrillium represents the interests of the people?'

Alex was finding it impossible to absorb everything that

had happened to him since he'd got up that morning. He didn't answer Carlos, but instead stopped dead.

'We're walking aimlessly. We need a plan.'

'We came to find Audra, right? Well, let's do that. We'd better take these helmets off – nobody is wearing them inside the building. This area looks like a medical facility. Audra was in a hospital gown of some sort when she recorded that video. Let's start checking the rooms.'

There was a moan and shout from further along the corridor.

Carlos removed his helmet, and Alex followed his lead.

'In here, come on.'

Alex was shocked by what he saw. Ten plastic tents, each with a person inside: three men, a toddler, a baby and five women. All were still, wired up to monitoring devices, with medical tools, syringes and vaccine bottles all around. The medical staff worked busily, barely noticing them stepping into the room.

'Can you see Audra?' Carlos whispered.

'This is a secure testing area. You shouldn't be in here.'

An officious man in a white coat had stepped forward. Alex didn't know what to say, but fortunately Carlos was prepared.

'Security sweep,' he said confidently. 'We had an incident at the gates. We're making sure everything is okay in here.'

'Yes, it is, no problems. Now please get out of this room.'

Behind him, a nurse was anxiously checking out the monitors by the baby's medical tent.

'Doctor?' she called.

'Which strain?'

'Same one as before.'

He cursed.

'Okay. Delete her and find another. Make sure you observe full cleansing protocols.'

The nurse keyed something into a terminal. There was a blue glow around the infant's body, then it was gone. The doctor turned to see Alex standing open-mouthed, staring at the empty tent where seconds ago a baby had been lying.

'Okay guys, I know it's your job to keep us all secure, but we're done here. And you didn't see that. I don't need to remind you of your oaths, right?'

'Of course not,' Carlos replied, still cool and in control. Alex was grateful for his friend's presence of mind. He was speechless. They quickly left the room.

'What the hell was that?' Alex asked. 'That baby vanished right in front of us. What are they doing here?'

'I have no idea, but I do know there's no way we'll be seeing that stuff on the newsreels. This must be where they test the vaccines. Things are even worse than we thought, Alex. The epidemic must be getting out of control. You know how frequent the VaXX programmes are now. Then there's the border controls, the grounding of flights, the change to localized government.'

'You're right. Something really big's going on.'

'Have you noticed there's suddenly more movement in these corridors?' said Carlos. 'I reckon things are hotting up. Harley must have raised the alarm. We need to move on. Hey, and Alex ...'

'What?'

'Try to act a bit cooler. You look like the guiltiest man alive. That's the quickest way to draw attention to us.'

'Alright, I get it,' Alex replied. 'But aren't you scared?'

'Terrified! But we've got to stay calm.'

Alex knew Carlos was right, but it was hard to control the fear that he felt. He'd give anything to be back home, in the security of the apartment. But he was beyond that now. He had to find out what had happened to Audra. And he had to check on his mum.

A voice cried out further along the corridor. Someone was in distress. They sounded broken, as if they'd lost the will to fight.

'Come on. Let's check that out,' said Carlos. 'That guy might be able to tell us more. Whoever he is, he doesn't sound very happy.'

They walked along the corridor, following the voice. They had left the medical zone now. Carlos tried the door.

'It's locked, and we don't seem to have access.'

The man inside shouted again, hearing the pushing and activity at the door.

'I need some water, please!'

It was an older man. His voice was weak, but he was well spoken. There was movement along the corridor.

'Shut your mouth! I'm sick and tired of hearing your whining.'

It was a Trooper, no helmet, but wearing full body armor and carrying a gun.

'You need some help in there?' Carlos said. He made it sound as if he and Alex had every right to be there.

'No, I'm good,' the Trooper replied. 'I'm going to give this idiot a kicking. He's been making that racket for the past two hours.'

'Yeah, I wondered what all the noise was,' Alex picked up, keen to show Carlos that he wasn't completely useless.

'Well, you can give him a kick for me,' said Carlos.

The Trooper walked up to the door. It opened up for him straightaway.

'It's the body armor that gives us access,' Carlos murmured, half to himself, half to Alex.

He rushed forward, pushing the Trooper through the open door. He crashed down on top of him, using his helmet to pound the Trooper's head.

Alex caught the door before it closed, and ducked into the room. He quickly looked around him. There were no windows. It was dimly lit by a single light fitting fixed to the ceiling. On the floor was a stained mattress. Beside it was a bucket, full and stinking. Where was the man who was inside the room?

The Trooper was now back on his feet, running at Carlos. Alex hadn't a clue what to do, so jumped on his back, his arm around his neck, squeezing tightly. The Trooper was thrashing around, trying to throw Alex off while pushing Carlos away from him. There was a loud crack and the Trooper fell to the floor, Alex still clinging to his back. He had been struck on the head by a length of steel. It looked like it had been smuggled in from elsewhere in the building; it didn't belong in this sparse room.

The occupant of the cell had been waiting by the door, ready to mount an ambush of his own. He was middle-aged, possibly even over sixty. He was wearing a gown similar to the one that Audra had been wearing in the video. He walked over to the Trooper, took his head in both hands, and gave it a sharp twist to the left. There was a sickening crunch as the vertebrae in his neck snapped.

Suddenly there was silence. The three of them looked at each other. The man spoke first.

'You had better be friends of Audra Woods, or I've just made the biggest misjudgment of my life.'

This time it was Alex's turn to talk.

'We are. I'm Alex, and this is Carlos. You know about Audra. She's alive?'

'She is,' the man replied. 'Or she was last time I saw her.

It was me who helped her to get that video out. I'm guessing that's why you're here?'

Alex nodded.

'Well, thank God for that!' he said, no longer speaking in the reedy voice he'd used to call out to the guard.

'Pleased to meet you, gentlemen. My name is Magnus.'

CHAPTER SEVEN

So this was Audra Woods. The world's best hope finally had a name and face.

Jasmine was trying to stop herself throwing up. She was used to treating those who had been wounded, maimed, appallingly disfigured, but always due to an accident, an act of terrorism or perhaps a natural disaster. Audra's mutilated body was the most shocking sight she'd ever seen.

Labatt knew he'd need to keep a close eye on her, now she'd seen the real reason for her presence at Fortrillium. Until recently Audra Woods had been a closely guarded secret, but to secure access to Professor Haworth, they'd been forced to share news of their potential breakthrough with other states. Now they had her with them in Sector 4, it was the last the other states would hear of her. Audra belonged to them now.

She was struggling to stay calm and in control.

'Is this necessary? Does it have to be done this way? If you kill her, you'll have nothing left.'

'It is necessary,' Labatt replied, looking over at Audra who now seemed aware that there were people in the room.

'This one is feisty. She's resisted us at every stage of our investigations. Under Sector 4's Emergency Schedule she's obliged to comply with all requests for medical analysis. She's contained like this for her own good.'

A ball of spit came flying out of Audra's mouth, landing on Labatt's shirt. He struck out at her, his fist punching her across the face. Her head dropped.

'You see! She fights me at every turn.'

He raised his voice so Audra could hear him.

'You will comply, Ms Woods. You are the most important person in this state and you will do as I wish.'

For somebody who had so casually inflicted harm, Labatt appeared disproportionately offended by the saliva running down his clothing.

'Take a good look around, Professor Haworth. Make a preliminary examination of the results on the console over there. I'm certain you'll agree this is exciting news.'

Labatt left the room. Jasmine was on her own with Audra. It was because of this young woman that she had been accosted and brought to Fortrillium.

'Who are you?' Audra mumbled, still unable to lift her head from the force of the blow. 'Another scientist come to poke and prod at me?'

'Wait, one moment.'

Jasmine scanned the room and quickly found what she was looking for. She prepared a syringe. Audra flinched as the needle approached her.

'This will take some of the pain away. I'm so sorry, this is not the way I would do it. I'll help you as much as I can.'

'There's nothing you can do.'

With a huge effort, Audra managed to raise her head to look at Jasmine.

'They have this place locked down. I tried to escape, and this is what they did to me.'

'There's a young man out there trying to get to you,' Jasmine whispered.

She didn't know how much time she had with Audra. Would they leave her alone with such a valuable test subject? She wasn't sure, she'd have to build up their trust.

'Alex?'

'Yes, I think that was his name. Alex. He was waiting by the gates when they brought me here. He risked a lot to try to get a message to me. Do you have people on the outside who could help you, Audra?'

'Only friends, but what can they do? They must have thought I was dead. I was abducted off the street one day. No warning, no fuss. It was a guy called Richter – if you think Labatt's bad, wait until you see him. He jumped out of a car as I was walking home from college, picked me up and threw me inside. That's it. I don't even know why.'

She was speaking rapidly, there was so much to tell and she didn't know how long they'd got before Labatt returned.

'I tried to escape. There's a man called Magnus—'

'You know Magnus?'

'Yes, Magnus is the one who gave me hope. The man's a genius.'

'Magnus is my husband. I'm Jasmine. I'm desperate to find him. Do you know where they're keeping him?'

Jasmine heard beeping. The keypad outside the room was being activated.

'No, I've no idea. I know he has a plan, but he wouldn't tell me in case they tried to torture it out of me. This is what they did to me after they caught ...'

The door opened. A woman in a white coat entered.

'We're preparing for the next round of tests. They begin

on the hour. Labatt's on his way. He wants you to take a look at that data.'

'Will do,' Jasmine replied.

She made a show of studying Audra and familiarizing herself with the tubes and electrical probes attached to her. Audra had hung her head again, making it look like she was out cold. She did that a lot, while hanging on to their every word. Whatever information she could glean, whatever clues there were about her situation, she wanted to know.

Jasmine knew she would have to trust the girl if she was going to find Magnus and escape. The woman in the white coat left them alone again.

'Can you hang on here, Audra? Are you strong enough?'

'I'm sick of it.'

Jasmine could see that. Her face was pale, her eyes dull.

'I want to scream when they come to me. I'm out of tears, I can't cry anymore. I want it to end.'

'I'm going to help you, and I need to find Magnus.'

'I haven't seen him since we sent the video out. We thought we were going to make it out of here, but they caught us. I don't know what happened to him—'

'Labatt's back!' Jasmine warned. She could hear the door being activated once again.

Audra hung her head while Jasmine made for the console. By the time Labatt was back in the room, now wearing a clean shirt, she was poring through the data. There were streams of it. And she found it all fascinating. For a minute she forgot about the human being that she'd been speaking to and saw the potential of the situation. Labatt saw that she'd instantly understood why the girl was so valuable.

'This is incredible!'

She looked up at him, speaking to him for the first time as a colleague, rather than the monster that he was.

'Is this all verified? Does The Global Consortium know?'

'No, The Consortium doesn't know, and they're not going to. This information could start a war. You must be able to see the value of it. If there are more like this test subject out there, it means we may have a chance of survival.'

'But how will you find out if you don't share the information? You can't keep it to yourself.'

'Now you're here, we don't need to share. We have the breakthrough, and we have your unique expertise. We can do this on our own. Only when we've secured our own state will we communicate it to the other Sectors, and then to our allies in the rest of the world. This is a chance to redraw the international landscape, a chance to destroy our enemies. If we lose this data to The Consortium, you realize what will happen: testing protocols, human rights legislation, trial periods. You and I both know that is not the way to save the population, Professor Haworth.'

Audra stirred. Jasmine looked at the girl, suddenly reminded of her humanity. She understood what Labatt was saying. In Sector 15 she'd railed against the President, urging him take more positive action. Magnus too had felt that sense of impatience, that some of the states simply hadn't grasped the seriousness of their situation. They'd reached Phase 6. This was the end. When every man, woman and child on the planet was at risk, did what happened to one individual matter?

Jasmine scanned the data again. Audra had a built-in resistance. Her records indicated she was several vaccines behind, yet the mutations that everybody else was experiencing – they simply weren't there. It offered the prospect of a natural immunity. If they could figure out why she was immune, they could find the cure. It was intoxicating to her.

But Audra was a human being – she had people who cared about her beyond the gates of Fortrillium. If they ever lost their humanity, there was not a lot of point saving the planet, they were not worthy of surviving as a species. She made up her mind there and then, as Labatt set to work to get his precious test subject ready for the next round of experiments.

She was getting them out of there. She was going to find Magnus, and they were going home. And Audra was coming with her.

'Deena? What are you doing here?'

The Trooper knew her. The weapon was lowered.

'It's Simone. Why are you here? They're searching all over for you.'

'I didn't know you'd become one of them, Simone. Just like Harley. A power kick.'

'It's not like that.'

Deena hated those helmets. They dehumanized.

'Can you remove that helmet please.'

'What's going on?' came Scorsese's voice from below.

'What *is* going on?' Deena asked.

Simone removed her helmet. She looked relieved. She didn't wear it well. She was self-conscious and awkward.

'Harley got me involved with the Youth Wing. I didn't want to. He's changed since he signed up to Fortrillium. I've seen a side of him that I didn't know existed.'

'Yeah, you can say that again.'

Scorsese pulled himself up and out of the opening to the sewer. Simone tensed and raised her weapon.

'It's okay,' Deena reassured her.

Simone looked terrified. She wasn't doing a good job of intimidating them. It was lucky she had the uniform to hide behind.

'These are my friends. This is Shane Scorsese ...'

'I know you, don't I? You're the politician guy.'

'Yes, that's me.'

Scorsese turned to help Evan out of the manhole, grabbing his good arm to haul him upwards. He was pale, consumed by pain. The wound was taking its toll.

'This is Evan Price,' Scorsese said. 'He's a soldier.'

Simone looked around, suddenly aware this was no casual chat with college friends.

'The place is crawling with Troopers. They shipped in us rookies. I got a call to join the search for fugitives. Please tell me that isn't referring to you, Deena?'

'It is. We're up to our necks in it. You remember Audra Woods, don't you?'

'Of course I do. It was terrible what happened to her.'

'What did happen to her?'

'Well ... she ... she disappeared, didn't she? She was abducted or something. Murdered even.'

'What if I told you she's still alive?'

'No ... that can't be possible.'

'Why not?'

Deena looked into her friend's eyes.

'Can I trust you, Simone? I never understood why you and Harley got together. I need to believe that the real you is still in there.'

Simone didn't seem sure what the answer would be.

She looked around, terrified that they'd be spotted and she'd be forced to make her choice.

'I hate this.' Her eyes teared up. 'I didn't want this, but Harley put my name forward. He can be very pushy. I got caught up in it. I want to break up with him, but I daren't. He seems to get more influence in Fortrillium every day. He ... he scares me.'

'Now is the time to pick which side you're on. We need your help, Simone. We have to get Evan to a doctor and we need to find a way to let people know what's going on. Can you escort us to Alex's apartment? His mum is the best person to talk to, she's high up in the authorities, she can help us—'

'Didn't you hear? It's not going to be that simple. That's why people like me got called in to help. All sorts of stuff is kicking off. They had a riot at City Park, there were shootings and arrests. Harley was there.'

'I've been predicting this for a long time. It's all coming to a head now,' Scorsese said. 'The city will break and there'll be rioting. And that's when we'll all discover the real purpose of Fortrillium.'

'I've seen it at the borders,' Evan joined in. 'It's happening already. Violence every day, people trying to get out, people trying to get in. It's a powder keg.'

'Simone, please. You've got to help us get to the apartment.'

'Okay,' she replied slowly. 'But I'll have to shake off my partner. He's trained and fully armed, so be careful. He sent me over here to keep me out of the way.'

'Leave that to me,' said Evan. He looked in no fit state to help anybody.

'Mrs Brady might not be there, though.'

Deena looked at Simone. They needed a break.

'Why not? Why won't she be there?'

'She was involved in the skirmish at the gates. Harley reckoned she'd been hurt. And you know she works for Fortrillium now?'

'No, I didn't know that, although Alex did say they'd been courting her. But she's still Susan Brady, whatever job she does. She won't let us down. She's our best hope.'

'We have to move fast,' said Simone. 'I have to be over at City Hall later this morning. There's some big announcement being made by President Henderson. They're shipping us all in for extra security.'

'City Hall is where we need to be,' said Scorsese. 'It's our chance to expose what's going on, in the full glare of the public eye. All the key figures will be there, and everything will be shown on live television—'

'Put your hands behind your heads!'

It was Simone's partner. His weapon was pointed at them.

'Simone, drop your weapon and place your hands behind your head. Now!'

Deena looked at Scorsese, as if to say *What now?* He shrugged slightly. As far as he could see, there was nothing they could do. The moment the Trooper requested backup, it was over.

The Trooper pointed his gun towards them and indicated that they should move towards the digger. They lined up in front of the vehicle. Deena looked at Evan, drawing his attention to where the Trooper was standing. The open manhole entrance was directly behind him.

Scorsese saw it too. The Trooper needed to radio for help. His weapon remained trained on the group, but he was distracted as he fumbled to activate the unit on his body armor. Scorsese saw his chance, rushing towards the

Trooper and pushing him backwards. He stumbled, losing his balance. Dropping his gun, he moved back to steady himself, but there was no ground beneath him. He fell awkwardly, and before he could stop himself he slid into the hole in the ground, banging his head against its solid rim as he disappeared into the darkness below.

Scorsese picked up the gun, anxious not to lose the advantage they'd won for themselves. There was a thudding sound and then a loud crack as the Trooper landed on the concrete below. He started screaming.

'I broke my leg! I broke my leg! Help me, please ...'

The group looked at each other.

A robotic voice sounded from the sewer.

Imminent danger of termination. This is now your final warning. Please evacuate the area immediately.

'Oh no, the machine's reactivated!' said Deena. 'We've got to get him out of there. We can't let that thing kill him.'

'Leave him,' Evan said.

'He's broken his leg, we're not leaving him.'

'He'd have killed us or handed us over to Fortrillium. Leave him.'

Please evacuate the area immediately.

'We are not leaving that thing to get him!' Deena shouted. 'We're not the same as them, okay? We're not the same!'

Simone was shining a torch into the manhole.

'Help me!' the Trooper shouted. 'I can't get up. Please help me. I wasn't going to hurt you. I have a family—'

Unauthorized personnel. This is a secure area. Under section 46.7v2 of the Fortrillium Sector 4 Security Directive, termination is now sanctioned by law.

'Hold my arm and lower me down there,' said Deena.

'You can't, Deena. The machine's too close to him,' said Scorsese.

'There's time if we're quick.'

Deena began to climb over the edge of the manhole cover, indicating that Scorsese and Evan should grab her arms and stay by the opening to haul them both out.

Please evacuate the area immediately.

She landed on her feet, by the side of the Trooper. His right leg was bent back awkwardly, he was almost passing out with the pain. His helmet was off now. Deena looked at his face in the torchlight. He was just a regular guy. Just like them.

'Help me! Please help me. I can't move. Please, get me away from that thing.'

Imminent danger of termination. This is now your final warning. Please evacuate the area immediately.

'Deena, come on, you have to leave him.'

'Can you stand? Can you take your weight?'

Deena looked up at the macerator. The blades were spinning more slowly, but it had started up again. It was almost upon them.

She tried to pull the Trooper up, but he let out a cry of pain.

'I can't stand, it hurts too much.'

'You have to. I haven't got the strength to lift you out—'

Imminent danger of termination.

'Deena, you have to leave him,' Scorsese shouted from above. 'You have to get out of there!'

The base of the macerator touched her foot and she pulled back immediately. Could they run deeper into the sewer and escape that way?

Imminent danger of termination.

'Deena, come on, you have to leave him!'

Evan and Scorsese's calls were increasingly desperate, their hands reaching down ready to haul her up.

She looked at the macerator and then at the Trooper. He was simply too heavy for her. Even if they tried to make their way further up the tunnel, it would only be a matter of time before they ran into one of those machines again.

'I'm sorry.'

She looked up towards Scorsese and Evan and jumped up so that they could catch her arms.

She pulled up her legs as the metallic rim of the macerator clipped her shoe.

'No! Don't leave—'

The Trooper's voice stopped dead. As Deena was hauled out to safety a spray of human debris shot out of the top of the open manhole cover, a severed hand landing on the ground at her feet. She began to weep, tears of frustration and despair. Simone gasped in horror.

'You did your best, Deena,' Evan said. 'You did your best.'

'So, the next thing is how to get out of here. In fact, how did you even get inside in the first place?'

Alex liked Magnus immediately. There was something about him, a confident and easy manner. He knew his face – he'd seen it in magazines, back when they had them, and on TV, usually newsreels. He was in tech, Alex knew that much. A mega geek and a very rich man. It was his technology and funded research that had resulted in so many people living such long and healthy lives. And here he was, a fugitive, like him and Carlos.

'It's a long story,' Carlos said. 'We have to act quickly.

They'll soon know we're in here – they might be on to us already. Do you know where Audra is?'

'Not exactly, but I have a rough idea which wing she's in. This place is vast, it seems to get bigger by the week.'

'We don't leave without Audra! That's more important than anything else.' Alex was determined to make it clear. 'I asked Professor Haworth to try and find her—'

'Whoa, hang on a moment! Jasmine is here? You mean she's in this building?'

'Yes, and it's the reason I'm here. I came to speak to her as she entered Fortrillium. Why, do you know her?'

'Jasmine Haworth is my wife! She must have come to find out what's happened to me. This was only supposed to be an advisory visit and it should have ended months ago. What's your plan, guys? I get that we need to find Audra and Jasmine and find some way out of here, but what will happen when we get beyond the walls of Fortrillium?'

Alex and Carlos looked at each other, embarrassed. Of course they didn't have a plan. They'd rushed into a hazardous, deadly situation with no thought as to how it might resolve itself.

'You do realize you'll have to leave Sector 4,' Magnus continued.

'I hadn't thought that far ahead,' Alex replied. 'But yes, I guess it's the only way. But my dad ... he's in prison. What about him?'

'You may have to make some difficult choices,' Magnus replied. 'There are some terrible things going on here, but I can assure your safety if we can get back to Sector 15. Although I can't even begin to imagine how we might do that.'

There was silence. The three of them looked at each

other, hoping someone might come up with a suggestion at least. Magnus took the lead.

'One thing is for sure. Whatever happens, we have to cross the state border. That means you two as well. Did you take your latest VaXX shot?'

'No, not me,' Alex replied. 'I was going to get it just before the deadline. Why?'

'Good, good. How about you?'

Magnus looked at Carlos.

'No, not me either,' Carlos replied. 'And I'm not intending to get it.'

'Okay, great. That helps us a little. The VaXX shots create a complication. It'll only be me to think about, and probably Jasmine too. I can fix that if I can get into the lab.'

'What's the problem with the VaXX programme?' Alex asked.

Magnus took a deep breath and looked at them both. Now was the time to tell the truth.

'The problem with the VaXX programme,' he said slowly, 'is that Fortrillium uses it as an instrument to control the population. They hijacked a piece of nanotechnology work I was doing and effectively weaponized it. We need to get to the lab so I can hack my way back in.'

He paused and eyed the dead man on the floor.

'Do you reckon I can squeeze into that uniform?'

He certainly had the wrong body shape for a Trooper. As he began to remove the clothes from the body, Carlos had a better idea.

'Isn't there an easier way? How about we escort you through the building. It'll make us look less obvious too.'

'You're probably right. But if we run into somebody who recognizes me, we're bound to get challenged. Kincade,

Richter, Labatt – those guys stalk this building like evil spirits. It's risky.'

'Let's use the cuffs on his utility belt,' said Alex. 'We don't need to lock them. If anybody asks, we're moving you somewhere safer after the security breach. How far is this lab?'

'Only a short distance away.'

Magnus grabbed at the cuffs and fitted them around his wrists, making sure that they could still be undone.

'Right, helmets on, guys. Let's give this a try.'

There was increased activity along the corridors, a sense of excitement and tension. Alex held up his weapon at a more assertive angle, keenly aware of how important it was that they should look the part.

Fortrillium was a labyrinth. Many of the vast, hangar-sized spaces weren't yet developed. It was a sinister work in progress. Magnus guided them along the corridors but suddenly halted. The coloured strip along the walls had turned from purple to red.

'This is wrong,' he cursed. 'I took a wrong turn up that last corridor. We need to go back.'

There was the sound of heavy boots clunking their way towards them.

'Troopers!' said Carlos. 'Quick, in here.'

They ducked through the nearest double doors, the security device on the door bleeping to confirm their access level.

'My God!' said Magnus. 'I haven't seen anything like this since ... well, for some time.'

'Since what?' Alex asked.

'I shouldn't have said anything. I can't tell you, Alex. That's something I can never discuss. Not even my wife knows. But I can tell you that this couldn't be more serious.'

The three fugitives looked out across the hangar. It was packed with modern, hi-tech and heavily armed helicopters, the like of which they'd never seen before.

'This is for land-based warfare,' gasped Magnus. 'I can't believe they have all this equipment here. I didn't know things were so far ahead—'

'What's going on?' Alex interrupted. 'We're not at war are we? Why does Fortrillium need all this stuff?'

'I don't have any answers, Alex. The rest of The Global Consortium doesn't have any idea about this. It's clear that Fortrillium's preparing for something, and whatever it is, it's not a peace mission.'

'This isn't good. We've got to get out of here,' said Carlos. 'My dad's seen choppers flying over the fields to the border. This isn't our city any longer. Like Magnus said, we have to get out of Sector 4.'

'Does either of you know how to pilot a helicopter?' Magnus asked.

Alex shrugged.

'Not me, man!' said Carlos.

'Look over there. There's a landing pad. These choppers can be flown out of the hanger. If we can fly one, that's our way out.'

'Not a chance!' Alex said. 'Come on, we need to get to that lab of yours, and I want to find Audra. Something's kicking off. There's too much activity in this place now.'

The Troopers had passed by. The immediate area was clear. As they stepped out into the corridor a siren began to sound.

'Looks like they already know I'm gone,' said Magnus.

'Either that or they've realized we're in here,' Carlos replied.

'Come on, let's go! The lab isn't far off now. If we can get there without being spotted, I think I can sort this thing.'

Magnus was rattled. He'd seemed calm and in control until that point. They raised their guns and followed him back up the length of the corridor. He was moving so fast it looked as if they were chasing rather than guarding him.

The sirens were urgent and penetrating. At last they arrived in front of a white door with the words *High Security – Authorized Personnel Only.*

'This is it, this is where I did my work. I can get to my equipment in there. You'll have to let me in,' he said. 'And you might have to deal with some staff in there. Try not to hurt them. They're decent people caught up in a bad place.'

'Ready?' Carlos asked, looking at Alex.

'Ready!' he replied.

Once again, their security levels allowed them through the electronic door. They burst in, with Magnus following behind. Waiting for them, casually smoking a cigar, was Richter, machine gun in hand, his finger resting on the trigger.

CHAPTER EIGHT

It had been a tense conversation over the secured Comms system. President Lance Henderson seemed to realize something was afoot. Even through his limited camera view he could hear that the alarms were sounding at Fortrillium HQ, their piercing ring like an angry mosquito unceasing in its quest for blood.

'All directives will have to be approved by me from now on, Kincade. The legislation will be amended. Is that clear?'

The President stared out of the console screen, his face red, his eyes narrowed in anger.

'It certainly is, Mr President, sir. And I wholeheartedly apologize if you feel I overstepped the mark in dealing with today's demonstration. As you know, it's imperative for state security that Professor Haworth got into the building safely. We had to ensure that at all costs.'

'You didn't need to slaughter innocent people. You used those drones to shoot the protesters. You didn't care who you killed or maimed – and all to keep order at a peaceful demonstration.'

Henderson spat the words, his voice shaking with rage.

Kincade hadn't thought the old man capable of making such an outburst. Even James Morgan, seated next to him out of view of the console camera, was taken aback.

'The weaponry and technology that has been assigned to Fortrillium is expressly for use in the advent of widespread civil breakdown,' the President continued. 'It is not a set of toys to play with as you wish, Mr Kincade.'

The alarms persisted in the background. As he glanced through the smoked glass of his office door and out into the corridor beyond, Kincade was growing anxious. What was going on? This day was going to be different from the rest. It was almost as if the alarms themselves had detected it.

Looking at the President's face on the screen, Kincade wondered if he'd even make it as far as the event at City Hall. If the old man had anything about him, he'd do them all a favour and die of a heart attack before his big speech. Chance would be a fine thing.

'Once again, Mr President, I can only apologize if you feel it was a misjudgment. The situation outside the gates was fluid. At one stage I thought they might abduct Professor Haworth. And you do understand how serious that would be, sir?'

He did understand the seriousness of that particular scenario. President Henderson had made his own pact with the devil. He realized they all had to play their part in the survival of mankind. But he was old fashioned and he believed in democracy and negotiation. As for Kincade, he was the sort of man who flourished in times of decay and disorder. He was a sociopath capable of turning on the charm, a spiteful, small man whose organizational skills and ability to get things done had seen his career soar.

The truth was, Henderson knew that men like Kincade were needed for what was coming. But he preferred him to work in the shadows. That way he wouldn't be forced to acknowledge – or deal with – the things Kincade had done. Henderson was determined to hang on to the appearance of humanity until forced to cast it aside. But now both men knew that the storm was almost upon them.

He decided to change the subject. He'd made his point.

'Are we all set for today?'

'Yes, everything is ready at City Hall. We've begun to erect larger screens around the city too. As infrastructure becomes more difficult to maintain, centralized means of communication will be essential.'

'At least we can agree on that. I'd like to accelerate work on the screens programme. If Professor Haworth is unable to pull a rabbit out of the hat, things are going to get very difficult extremely fast.'

'I'll make sure it's done, sir. We will have full TV and radio coverage in Sector 4, but rural areas will only have it streamed to them to contain the reach of your broadcast. The network of screens will help us to control who sees what. I strongly advise against letting these broadcasts be seen out of state.'

'We'll record a second address afterwards. Something that we can let the rest of the world see. You're right, Kincade. We need to start tightening up on who sees what. Right, everything seems in order. I'll see you at City Hall at midday. You're bringing Labatt and the girl?'

'Yes. We may not need the girl, but if we do, we'll have her on hand. I haven't had time to speak at any length to Haworth yet, but Labatt will make sure she's on message.'

President Henderson nodded. Kincade's screen went blank. He turned to the man next to him.

'What do you think?'

Morgan smiled.

'Easy,' he replied. 'We'll make a great team.'

'Has Labatt got the girl ready? She looked terrible last time I saw her. That man really should try to work more tidily.'

'He assures me that all tissue damage areas will be concealed by clothing. She'll be sedated too. We can't risk any outbursts.'

'How about Susan Brady? Do you think she'll play ball?'

'I fast-tracked her promotion paperwork – she started this morning. I've also got her involved in today's little pantomime. She won't know what's going on until it's too late.'

'You're certain she'll come onside?'

'If she wants to see her husband again, she'll do whatever's necessary. And we believe her son was caught up in the riot outside the gates today. If we can confirm that, we'll have her over a barrel.'

'Isn't he friends with the girl ... Audra?'

'Yes, they were boyfriend and girlfriend. I'd say we'll have Susan Brady well and truly stitched up after today. With that much leverage over her family, she'll never dare to make a move.'

'Great! It just keeps getting better. What was the son up to? Anything we need to worry about?'

'No, I spoke to Richter earlier, and he dismissed it as youthful political exuberance, nothing we need to get anxious about. Brady will be good, she knows her stuff. She's scrupulously honest and thorough. Once we have her in our pocket, she'll be perfect for the job.'

'This is good, James. Well done. After today we'll be able to get things moving. We've floundered in this wilderness of Henderson's for far too long. Now we have

Haworth, it's all falling into place. Once we show our hand, there's no going back. I want you by my side. I believe you're the man for the job.'

'I'm with you, sir. It's an honour. You know how long I've wanted to get into politics. Things are changing fast. It's all about survival and I mean to make sure this state survives, whatever happens to the others. I'll do whatever it takes.'

'You've thought through every detail of the President's address? We need to allow him to get about a third of the way through. I don't want to have to show the girl if we don't have to. I want Haworth to be the one to set out our stall.'

'It's all in hand, sir. If he sticks to his schedule – and Brady will make certain he does – it'll run like clockwork.'

Kincade looked at Morgan and congratulated himself on finding such a worthy companion. Morgan was ambitious and realistic, and he shared his view of the world. It would take extreme measures, but between them, they would ensure the security of the state. A man like Henderson was too old-fashioned and conventional.

'You'd better go and check out why those alarms are going off, James. Today is not the day for any further interruptions. If everything works out, by tonight we'll have full control over the state. And you, James Morgan, are going to make an excellent new President.'

It took some time for Deena to calm down. Only days before, she and Simone had been college rivals. There wasn't much love lost between them, they simply existed in different orbits. But now they'd been brought together, both terrified by what was happening, caught up in events they could never have imagined.

As Scorsese helped her to wipe the remains of the Trooper from her clothing, and as she struggled not to throw up for a second time, Deena had to face the full horror of their situation. There was no way back now. Fortrillium was evil, it was no force for good.

Now she realized how close she'd been to getting caught in the web when Audra disappeared. And she understood – finally – that Audra hadn't been murdered or run away. Perhaps, deep down, she'd always known that Fortrillium had taken Audra. Audra had been abducted because of what they'd discovered in that newly built sewer.

Had the macerators been put there after they'd captured her? They hadn't been there a year ago. That would make sense. Fortrillium was an organization that was prepared to kill to keep its secrets. They had to find out what had happened to her. Deena couldn't go back to the children's home – if she'd ever felt rootless before, it was going to be even worse now. She didn't know where to begin.

Scorsese took the lead and she was grateful for it.

'We need to get some medical attention for Evan. And we have to find a way to get into that meeting at City Hall. It's time to blow this thing wide open.'

Simone hesitated. Like Deena, she was running through the options in her head. Could she lie? Claim that she'd been overpowered in a fight and that Deena and her new friends had been responsible for the death of her part-ner? It wouldn't take them long to connect her with Deena. And Harley had become so changeable since signing up with Fortrillium that she wasn't sure she trusted him now. She'd joined the Youth Wing as a trainee to try to appease him. But she didn't like the environment and she was beginning to doubt that she'd like Harley for much longer.

'I'm really scared,' she said. 'I want to go home.'

This sparked something in Deena.

'You can't walk away from this!' she shouted.

Her sudden anger surprised them all. She'd been shaken and sickened by what had happened to the Trooper, but now she was ready to start fighting back.

'You can try to blame us if you want, Simone, but you saw what happened. I tried to save him. I didn't want that Trooper dead any more than I want anyone else dead. I don't want any of this. But we are where we are. We're right in the middle of it.'

Simone was silent and chastened.

'You remember Audra Woods?' Deena asked her. 'Remember all the BS about her being murdered or abducted? Well, maybe she was, but you know who did it, don't you? It wasn't some madman roaming the city streets. It was Fortrillium. They destroy anyone who stands in their way. We have to stop them – before it's too late.'

'I couldn't have put it better myself,' said Scorsese. 'We need to go to City Hall and challenge the President. It has to be in public with the TV cameras there. We have to call them to account. So far, Fortrillium has been working in the shadows. They have to be forced out into the open. People must understand what's going on.'

Evan had been quiet, preoccupied with his wounds. At last, he spoke.

'I agree. It has to be City Hall. We don't have long until the President's speech begins. How dense are the deployments of Troopers in this neighbourhood?'

For a few seconds, Simone didn't speak. She was about

to switch sides, and she needed to give it a final run-through in her head. She consulted a device on her wrist.

'The number of Troopers has decreased considerably since we were dispatched. They must have given up searching for you. They'll all be gathering at City Hall. I can guide you to Alex's.'

'Okay, let's go!'

Scorsese was keen to commit everybody while there was a consensus of opinion.

Simone carried her weapon and kept her helmet on, walking slightly behind the main group so she could claim to have detained them if they ran into trouble. She wasn't entirely convinced that she wouldn't hand them straight over to Fortrillium and blame them for everything if they did meet any patrols. She knew what she ought to do, but would she be strong enough to follow her conscience?

The journey to Alex's apartment was without incident, but there was a spark of electricity in the air. The President's address was long overdue. The citizens had known for a long time that something serious was going on, but nobody knew what it was. Some form of explanation was required. The expectation was that they'd know by noon, with just half a day to go until the deadline for the latest VaXX programme.

'I didn't get my VaXX!' Deena suddenly remembered. 'I meant to get it done. I won't have time now.'

'Deena. You're on the run from Fortrillium. I suspect it's now immaterial.'

Scorsese was smiling as he spoke. But Deena had spent a lifetime following the rules. Her impulse was towards guilt and obligation. She reproached herself for having turned away from the queue when she'd been waiting with Alex and Carlos. She should have had it done there and then, as Simone and Harley had, but once her friends had left her she'd drifted away, losing interest.

They arrived at the door to Alex's apartment. From the other units on the same floor came the sounds of flat screens broadcasting the build-up to the President's address. The entire city was getting ready. Scorsese knocked, quietly, not wanting to draw any other residents out onto the landing.

They heard a shuffle inside. Scorsese knocked again. The door opened. It was Susan Brady, still in uniform, her arm bandaged. She swiftly surveyed their faces: a Trooper, a badly bloodied soldier, a man she recognized from some-where – a politician, she thought – and Deena, a familiar face.

'My God, Deena— '

'Is Alex here?'

'No, something ... something serious has happened. What on earth have you been up to?'

Susan Brady knew it wasn't Deena's blood that was drying on her jacket. She also knew that the soldier hadn't got his wounds tripping down the stairs.

'Come in. Get off the landing.'

She closed the door behind them. Scorsese – ever the politician – introduced himself.

'I thought I knew you. You're the guy who's been campaigning for greater transparency in the new gover-nance system. I've seen your name come up in a couple of official documents recently. You're not very popular, but I take it you know that?'

'You're right on both counts, Mrs Brady.'

Deena was in no mood for pleasantries.

'Where's Alex?' she asked. 'I need to speak to Alex. It's about Audra.'

'That's why I'm here,' Susan replied. 'I have to head

over to City Hall shortly. I came home to freshen up after getting this dressed at the hospital.' She touched her bandaged arm. 'Alex has got himself caught up in some trouble. I was scanning the reports on my console when you knocked. I saw him in the crowd earlier – there was a riot – they shot people. I've never seen anything like it. They were my people, but I didn't order that—'

'Is he hurt?' Deena interrupted, anxious for her friend.

'He got away, as far as I can tell. There's no record of him in the official reports, dead or arrested. But what was he doing there? He said nothing to me.'

'Alex was looking for Audra, I'm sure of it. We think ... *I* think she's alive. Whatever's happened to her, it's Fortrillium that's responsible.'

'What have I done?' Susan said, thinking out loud. 'Today's my very first day of working for this damned organization. What I've seen already ... what you're telling me. Who are these people?'

'Nobody knows,' said Scorsese. 'But I think we're about to find out. We have to get to City Hall and speak directly to the President himself. Today is the day we blow the lid off this thing.'

Susan and Deena looked at each other. There was still somebody who mattered more to both of them than what was going on at City Hall.

'What about Alex?' they asked in unison.

They stopped dead in their tracks. So this was it. They knew who Richter was, a mercenary who'd aligned himself with Fortrillium.

'Close the door, and sit down,' Richter said, his gun trained directly at them. 'Weapons over there.'

He indicated a workstation where he wanted their equipment to be placed. As Carlos went to sit on one of the office chairs that had been set out for them, he shouted, '*Everything*, Matiz!'

Carlos returned to the table and placed a sinister-looking scalpel on it.

Alex looked at him as he sat down next to him.

'I picked it up in that medical area,' Carlos muttered. 'You know I prefer knives to guns.'

'Okay, to business,' Richter started. 'You guys are in big trouble. I assume you know who I am?'

He took the silence as his confirmation.

'So, here's how it is. You three need to get out of here, but I can tell you that you won't get far. We know who you are and the entire building has been scrambled to try to find you.'

As if on cue, a Trooper burst through the door, ready to check the area for the fugitives. Richter stayed calm and looked directly at the man as he scanned the room, attempting to work out what was going on. The moment the door shut properly, Richter raised his gun and shot the Trooper through the heart. He dropped to the ground.

Alex flinched. He'd already seen too much death for a lifetime. Carlos leaped up to snatch his scalpel.

'Steady!' Richter barked. 'Sit back down and listen to me. We don't have long before they realize we're here.'

Alex glanced at Magnus. He could almost hear his mind working away. He didn't seem troubled by Richter or the death of the Trooper. For a man whose intellect was geared to science and technology, he seemed remarkably calm in the face of adversity.

'I want to get out of Sector 4,' Richter said.

No one answered. They didn't know what to say.

'This place is going to burn very soon. It's time for me to leave. In fact, we're leaving together.'

'What are you talking about?' Carlos hissed. 'You're a butcher. We're not going anywhere with you.'

'I'm a hired hand and I do what it takes to survive. Just like you did, Carlos, when you sliced off the heads of Troopers Stewart and Marshall. Yes, I know about that. It's in the sit-rep already. Did you know that both those Troopers had families to go home to? Did you also know that three months ago they were part of Sector 4's finest police force? They were doing what they had to – the same as us.'

Alex found his courage at last.

'But why do you need us?'

'Nobody gets out of Sector 4 alive,' Richter replied. 'Have you had the latest VaXX yet? I have. And, as Magnus over there will tell you, it's his little invention that will kill you if you try to leave Sector 4.'

They looked at Magnus. He hadn't been paying attention, his mind was quite clearly elsewhere, but he'd heard his name.

'Is that right, Magnus? What have you done?'

'It's half correct,' Magnus replied, studying Richter's face, trying to work out where he was going with this. 'The original use for the nano-devices was for something ... well, it was for something completely different. Unknown to me, Labatt was monitoring my studies and has adapted them to his own purposes. They've created a killing machine in that new VaXX programme. They can effectively annihilate – delete – anybody at will. They're going to need it too, when they finally reveal what's going on.

'The entire planet is on the verge of being wiped out by a deadly plague. And I'm partly responsible for it. It was me who created the conditions where ...'

He paused and thought for a moment before continuing.

'Let's just say, the plague is not from this world. It was brought to us. It's been metamorphosing for several years now. We thought it was a new strain of flu, but each incarnation becomes more virulent. That's what the VaXX programmes are about. We've been trying to keep ahead of it, but we're losing the battle. A couple more mutations and I don't think we'll be able to cope with it any longer. We're already at Phase 6 in terms of infection. It's a matter of which mutation finishes us all off now.'

There was silence while the information sank in. It made sense. The VaXX programmes had become increasingly urgent. At first, they were advisory, but for many months now they'd been compulsory. There were dire warnings of the consequences of not being vaccinated – death among the very young, the elderly and the infirm. In spite of a succession of impressive medical advances, this deadly illness appeared to be like the common cold, something they simply couldn't cure.

Two more Troopers burst through the door. This time Richter didn't wait for it to close. He shot them as they entered, barely taking his eyes off Magnus.

'Carlos, move the bodies clear of the door, please. So, Magnus, my question to you is: can you remove the nano-devices that were delivered in the latest VaXX shot? I'm going nowhere unless you can. If you can't, and I have to stay here, I'm handing you over to Fortrillium and I'll have to take my chances with Bryce Kincade.'

'I can do it, but I need a little time. They're going to

have us surrounded soon. We'll never get out of this building, it's like a fortress.'

'Leave that bit to me,' Richter said calmly. 'All I want to hear from you is that you can neutralize the devices.'

Magnus nodded. 'I can, and Labatt knows it can be done. Of course, there's no way he and Kincade will have those things injected into their bodies.'

He looked at Alex and Carlos.

'What about you guys? Did you have the latest VaXX?'

They'd dragged the Troopers out of the way and sat back down on their chairs. It amazed Alex how quickly he had become accustomed to the sight of a dead body.

'No, we're safe. Neither of us had it,' Alex said.

Things were moving fast. He had to speak out before it was too late.

'We don't leave without Audra!' he demanded, his voice shaking with emotion. 'I'm not risking all this and leaving without her. And I need to take care of my mum, she's had the VaXX.'

'Okay, we're a team, time for a group hug,' Richter sneered. 'Magnus, I have your console and the contents of that locked drawer you had concealed in your desk. Is that all you need?'

'Is it okay if I walk over to my workstation?' Magnus asked. 'There are a couple more things I need to get. I've been in a situation like this before. I know how it works. I know what has to be done.'

Alex wondered what he was talking about. He seemed to be reliving something from his past.

'Can I call my mum?' Alex asked. 'I want to make sure she's safe.'

'Sure, kid.'

Richter threw over an electronic device. 'It's secure,

though your mother's line won't be. Be careful what you tell her. You may want to say your goodbyes.'

'How are we going to get Audra?' Carlos asked. 'And how will you get us out of here?'

'He doesn't get his nano-device neutralized until he does,' Magnus said, returning with a small bag of equipment. 'You get us out of this place, Richter, and I neutralize you immediately. Fair?'

'Yes, Magnus, I get it.'

Richter had read Magnus's file. He wasn't going to argue. This man knew exactly what he was doing.

'Okay, Magnus, let's start with your lady, the professor. Matiz, you need to act as if Magnus is your captive. Pick up your gun from over there and look like you mean it. Try and find the professor, if you can, and then meet us at the hangar. We'll meet up at Yellow Zone, Warehouse B.'

Carlos swung Magnus's bag over his shoulder and went to grab his gun. As he did so, his hand hovered over the scalpel. Should he kill Richter there and then? Could the man be trusted? He thought about it. Richter had skin in the deal, he was as vulnerable as they were. Fortrillium could use the nano-device to delete him too. Besides, if Richter was serious about getting out of the state, he would be a great ally. Carlos picked up the scalpel anyway and concealed it in his waistband. He and Magnus left the room.

'Right, let's find your girlfriend and get out of this hellhole,' Richter said, turning to Alex who had just finished his call.

The teenager's face was pale. Something was up.

'You spoke to your mother?'

'Yes. She says she's heading to City Hall for the President's address. She's with my friend Deena and some others. They're in trouble. I told Mum about the helicopters here. She said that was the best way for us to escape from Fortrillium. We can land on the helipad on the roof of City Hall. The last thing they'll expect is for us to access it from the air because all non-military flights are blocked now. If we can make it there, maybe we can all get out together.'

James Morgan was agitated by the persistent ringing of the alarms. He was so close to the presidency now, he wasn't going to let anything stand in his way. Yet this must signify a security breach, perhaps even another protest outside the gates. Whatever it was, it needed to be quashed – and fast.

He checked his gun and stepped into the corridor from Kincade's office. The first person he saw was Harley, who'd joined the search parties flooding through Fortrillium. Morgan liked Harley Lydell. He was someone who instinctively saw what had to be done and would help to achieve it without question. He would go far. He was just the sort of young person that Fortrillium needed.

'Harley, I hadn't expected to see you here. I was disappointed to see the alert involving you earlier. What was that all about?'

'It was a misunderstanding. We've got an intruder in here and I know who it is: a kid from college called Carlos Matiz. He planted a knife on me as I was entering the building. I'm the one who raised the alarm.'

Morgan checked his pocket console and saw that

Harley was telling the truth. The security flag on him had been lifted. There was an intruder – possibly multiple intruders – inside Fortrillium.

'What's he like this guy Matiz? He's not related to the Matiz family who farm the cabbages is he?'

'That's him. They're rich. He's always going on about how the government is out to get his dad. He's paranoid, he doesn't understand how the world is changing.'

Morgan gave a small smile. He'd signed an order the previous day authorizing the state takeover of farming outputs. Carlos's concerns would be vindicated. It was the natural evolution of a militarized government. Ultimately, if food continued to flow through the shops and onto tables, nobody would care what happened to people like Luis Matiz.

'I'm pleased to hear you haven't landed yourself in trouble. You've done good work for Fortrillium, Harley. I see great things ahead of you – particularly after today. Are you going to City Hall?'

'Yes, I'm part of a security detail, but we've been diverted to find the intruders. We know there are two of them. Carlos has to be with Alex Brady or Deena Jakobson – probably Alex. I saw Deena last night, she was on her own.'

He smirked as he remembered how they'd intimidated her. That's what he loved about Fortrillium. When you were in that uniform, you could do what you wanted. He relished the power it gave him, the way people squirmed when he gave them orders. He'd got respect working for the organization. He and Simone could go far together.

'You want to come with me?' Morgan asked. 'Let's see if we can find these people. Watch me and learn.'

'For the record, Carlos isn't my friend. He's someone I

have to put up with at college. It would be my pleasure to see the end of the little toad.'

'That's the spirit.'

Morgan headed along the corridor with Harley following.

'Alex Brady ... can you confirm that he's related to Susan Brady, Harley?'

'The cop? Yes, that's her. She's high up in the police. Didn't stop her husband getting locked up though.'

'Yes, I do know that family. Susan Brady's working for Fortrillium now. So you think her son might be with this guy Carlos?'

'They come as a team: Deena, Carlos and Alex ... and Audra at one time, but she disappeared.'

'Harley, wait here for a minute.'

James Morgan had moved up the ranks of Fortrillium so fast because he was good at making connections. He was also adept at taking the right action at the appropriate time. He walked further along the corridor, out of earshot. Harley was an impressive young man, but there were still some strategic issues that had to remain private.

Harley watched as Morgan made his call, his ears pricking up at the word Brady. He tried to page Simone. There was no reply. Perhaps she was in a class. Members of the Youth Wing were allowed to attend college when they weren't needed by Fortrillium. That suited Harley, as they were guaranteed their credits however little work they did. That meant that not only was he able to cover up his academic failings, but he'd also increased his status among the other students. That's what people like Carlos and Alex didn't get.

'Okay, let's see if we can find these friends of yours, shall we?'

There was heightened activity in the corridors. Troopers moved purposefully throughout the building while sirens rang out persistently, warning lights flashing at every turn.

Harley loved the nods of deference to Morgan as they made their way through the labyrinth.

'Where the hell is Richter?' Morgan frowned. He'd been trying to raise him via the Comms gear, but with no luck.

Harley had never met Richter, but he'd heard about him and seen his face on the flat screen. He was a war hero. He was another one who got things done. The prospect of actually meeting the man was exciting.

Morgan stopped dead in the middle of the corridor. At last everything was connecting. Now he could see what was about to happen. It was a moment of realization. He turned to Harley.

'This is all going to turn to dust if I don't take things into my own hands. I'm trusting you, Harley. This is your chance to prove I'm right about you. I want you to go to the cells and find a man called Michael Brady. Make sure he's properly secured and bring him to City Hall.'

He intercepted two passing Troopers.

'Do you know who I am?'

'Yes, sir.'

'I want you to go with Harley. You must follow his orders to the letter. Do either of you have transport privileges?'

'Yes, I do,' the taller of the two responded.

'Harley, you need to take transportation and use it to move the prisoner to City Hall. Meet me there. Don't let me down.'

An intoxicating rush of adrenalin electrified Harley's

body. He was in charge of two Troopers. He had a crucial mission. And on top of all that, it was Alex's dad he was transporting. The day couldn't have got any better.

Morgan sent them on their way, and stopped for a moment to consider his planning. It was like a game of chess, contemplating the various moves and what results they might produce. His gut instincts had always served him well. He only had fragments of information at his disposal, but he could see what was coming.

He considered what Alex and Carlos would do next. The requisitioning of farmland had been actioned at dawn and Carlos's family would likely be dead by now. When he found out what had happened to them, Matiz would want revenge. Alex must have come looking for his father – and probably his girlfriend. And then there was Susan Brady. Perhaps she wasn't the strength they'd thought her to be. When it came to it, she would always put her son first.

Susan Brady was orchestrating President Lance Henderson's keynote address at City Hall. She didn't know it, but she was actually in charge of nothing. Together with Kincade and a small group of loyal Troopers, James Morgan would change the course of history that day.

A shiver of excitement ran down his spine. The Brady family had just given him the perfect plot twist. He could have them all there – Susan, Alex and Michael – and they would go down in history as the terrorists who were to blame for it all. The entire state would despise the Brady family for what they'd done, plotting to assassinate President Lance Henderson, the well-respected politician.

The final pieces were being moved into position. Henderson's death would result in the meteoric rise of James Morgan to President. Checkmate.

Susan Brady had been forced to make some difficult decisions in her life. The first time she killed a man was while she was on foot patrol. He drew his gun on her and didn't respond to her pleas to put down his weapon. She shot, in self-defence, and changed her life for ever.

When Alex was born, she'd had to choose which twin would survive. The medics had informed her that it was one of the babies or neither of them. She'd chosen Alex over his twin brother Oliver – Alex was stronger and fighting harder. They'd never told him that, it was too heartbreaking. Susan had had to live with that decision and every day Alex's presence reminded her of it.

She was now faced with a similar dilemma. She fully understood its consequences. It would change everything, there would be no going back. They had to make a choice – leaving it for another day was not an option.

'You know what this means?' she said to Deena, looking her directly in the eye. 'You will have to leave the home, your friends, the carers – everything. You can't say goodbye either. You'll be walking away from your life. Are you sure you want to do it?'

'I'm with Alex,' she replied. 'There's nothing for me here. Last night I ran into Harley and his mate, and I saw exactly how things are going to be. The bullies will run the state.'

She paused and looked across at her friend standing in her Trooper's uniform.

'I'm sorry, Simone.'

A small tear rolled down Simone's cheek. She knew Deena was right, but she didn't have her courage.

'I can't leave Sector 4. My parents are here, Harley is here ... I can't just walk away.'

'You have to be comfortable with your choices, Simone,' Susan said gently. She knew it wasn't easy for the girl.

She turned to the men.

'What's the endgame for you, Mr Scorsese?'

'I'm going to stay in the city and fight for a different political model. I don't have family – I only have myself to think about. I have to stay.'

'And you?' Susan asked, looking at Evan. 'What's your story?'

She could see he was tense. He was less certain of what he was fighting for.

'I'm with Scorsese,' he replied eventually. 'We have to create a different future. Things can't stay the way they are.'

There was a hollowness about the way he spoke. They seemed like empty words coming from him.

Susan looked around the apartment. Alex's call to her Comms unit had been hurried, he was scared and he'd garbled out the plan. If it had been one of her officers running her through a raid, it wouldn't have seemed quite so incredible. But this was her son, her precious son Alex, talking her through the most amazing escape plan. She'd run her fair share of complex operations in her time, but never with her own child at the centre of it.

Alex was in Fortrillium as a fugitive, and that alone was enough to seal his fate, she knew that. Carlos too. Their plan was to break out Audra and Professor Haworth, the very person she'd been responsible for escorting to the secure base that same morning. He'd babbled something about disease and human testing, she could barely take it in. And here was Deena, a young woman she loved dearly, telling her much the same.

The world was broken. And she'd just signed a contract that had her supping with the devil. She thought about her husband. Where was he?

If only they could get him out too. But if it came to making a choice, she had to choose her son, she had to choose Alex.

Susan looked around the apartment with all its reminders of Alex. Would that rushed call from inside Fortrillium be the last chance she'd have to speak to him? It was time to put the plan her son had communicated to her in place.

'I need to leave for City Hall. We'll go together. Down to the basement car park, everyone.'

They checked their weapons. The conversation was minimal. Simone had gone on ahead of them. She'd promised not to betray them, and they had to believe her. She was scared, she'd intervened as much as she dared. She'd already have some explaining to do about her dead companion back at the sewer. Susan had told her to lie, claim they'd become separated in a chase and that she'd lost her Comms device. Without proof, they couldn't implicate her in anything.

As she left, Susan slipped a photo out of a frame on the hall table and folded it to a suitable size for her pocket. It showed her, Alex and Michael in happier times. She was doing this for her family.

'Get in the van!' she instructed when they reached the dimly lit basement garage. 'Keep your heads down. You mustn't be seen. The minute I start to see Troopers on the streets, I'm dropping you off and you'll have to make your own way to City Hall. When you get there, head for the Blue Zone public standing area. Ditch your weapons, security will be strict. Deena, when you see me moving from the security area follow me out, but if we get separated, head for the helipad on the roof.'

There was very little traffic on the roads. The ride through the city gave an eerie chill of expectation. They passed one of the newly erected screens. Newsreel images were being displayed on it and a crowd had gathered to watch.

Susan swung into a side street and stopped the vehicle.

'This is it, you're on your own now.'

She paused.

'Good luck, everybody.'

Evan, Scorsese and Deena got out of the vehicle. As Susan drove off, Deena suddenly felt alone.

They disposed of their guns in a nearby skip. Deena shivered. She felt naked without her weapon. Evan drew up the hood of his jacket to hide his face. Meanwhile, Deena took off her blue woolen hat and gave it to Scorsese who pulled it down over his grey hair. He took his reading glasses out of his pocket and put them on. Such a rudimentary attempt at disguise, but it worked.

Flags ran down the full height of the facade of City Hall. These were the black flags of Fortrillium, a red 'F' emblazoned across the centre of each. The three of them joined the crowds filing into the building. Without their weapons, they filtered through security unchallenged.

There was a large screen set up at the front of the stage ready to project the President's face. The audience was being herded into colour-coded areas, VIPs and politicians in the yellow and orange zones, the public in the blue and red zones. TV cameras were stationed around the interior arcade area. Small groups of state dignitaries were in the balcony sections, which also held armed security teams and the occasional TV camera. There was a buzz of expectation in the air, everybody guessing what the President would say in his address.

Deena looked over to the security bay and saw that Susan had taken her place. Where was Evan? Deena scoured the area. He was nowhere to be seen. Scorsese was standing close by, poised to intercept the President as soon as he arrived in the hall. Henderson was a genial man, he always liked to stop and shake hands. Scorsese knew this would be the time to catch him.

Deena looked back towards Susan. What was going on? Two Troopers wearing red armbands were escorting her away from her station, on her face a look of confusion. Then she heard Evan's voice, no longer in the crowd but standing in the aisle a few steps away, next to two more Troopers wearing red armbands. He was pointing at them.

'That's them over there. Shane Scorsese and Deena Jakobson. They haven't got any weapons!'

Deena felt a firm grip on her arm and realized at once their mistake. They'd taken Evan at face value, never even thinking that he was anything else but sincere. But he'd led them into a deadly trap.

'James Morgan knows how to screw up an escape plan!' Richter scowled, reading his mobile device. He finished off his cigar and stubbed it out on the floor. 'This is going to take some doing.'

He picked up his gun and slid it into its holster.

'What's happened?' Alex asked.

'Your girlfriend is being moved to City Hall. They're taking Jasmine Haworth too. Those friends of yours had better not mess this up. If I didn't need that Magnus guy to vouch for me in Sector 15, I'd be leaving on my own.'

Alex remained silent. He didn't like this man, but he was their only chance of getting out of Fortrillium.

'I'll check in with Morgan,' Richter continued. 'I'll try to throw him off the scent. He wants me over at City Hall.'

He typed a text and sent it to Morgan.

'There, I've told him I'm dealing with a problem in the prison.'

He looked at Alex and grinned.

'Put your helmet on, kid. We're going for a ride.'

Navigating the corridors with Richter was a different experience from the way they'd fumbled around earlier. He knew where he was going. With this formidable killing machine at his side, Alex went completely unchallenged. They arrived at the underground shuttle and Richter indicated that Alex should step inside the waiting train.

'You ever seen any gun action?' Richter asked, as they were propelled through the tunnel towards their destination.

He glanced at Alex.

'No, I see you haven't. Okay, there's going to be some shooting. I'm going to find you a keycard and you need to open up the cells. That's all you have to do. Open the cells and meet me back at the shuttle.'

The train drew up at a platform. They got out and Richter walked him confidently through the security gates and into a vast domed area. As Alex took in the size of the place, Richter turned round and shot the four guards who were manning the security gates. They were all slumped on the floor before Alex had even realized what was going on. Richter had used some kind of silencer and the small sound the gun had made was drowned out by the hubbub coming from the cells. Richter could see Alex's fear.

'You need to stay nice and steady. There's worse to come. Wait for my signal.'

Richter handed Alex a keycard he'd taken from the security guard. He then moved towards the office where a man was working at a console. He crept behind him, clamped his huge hands to either side of the man's head, and with a sharp twist to the left snapped his neck.

He didn't pause to look at the corpse of the man he'd so brutally murdered, but ran back out and scanned the tower dominating the centre of the cavern. He had moved so fast, the guards on lookout were unaware of what had been happening below. He left Alex at the base and bounded up the steps two at a time.

This time Alex heard the shots. Five of them. The man was merciless. Richter was gesturing from the top of the tower. It was Alex's signal.

There was a ripple of expectation among the prisoners in their cages. He grabbed the keycard and started to open the cell doors.

'Let us out!'

'What's going on? Are we free?'

'Is it over? Please tell me it's over ...'

Then, a familiar voice.

'Alex? Is that you?'

'Dad?'

The inmates were surging around him, it was hard to distinguish one from the other. Their clothes were damp and dirty, their emaciated bodies covered in sores.

A man stepped out of the crowd. His beard was long and straggly, his clothing torn and stained.

He placed his arms around Alex, hugging him tightly.

'Alex! What's going on? What are you doing here?'

'Dad … Is it really you? We thought you were being held in—'

Ahead of them came a loud crashing sound. Richter was throwing the weapons taken from the guards onto the floor from the tower. He was creating a diversion, making weapons available to the inmates, giving them the means to fire at any Troopers they might encounter while making their escape.

There was anger in the air. The inmates wanted blood.

'Alex, we have to keep moving. Do you have a plan to get out? Is that man up there with you?'

'Yes, he's going to take us to Mum and then he'll help us get out of the state. We've got a safe place to go.'

'You trust him?'

'No, not really, but I'm not certain we have any other choices. He wants out of here the same as us. He's our best bet.'

The inmates were crowding through the security gates, which had now been fully opened. They were waiting for one of the shuttles to complete its circuit so that they could exit through Fortrillium. It was the only way out.

Richter was back, he'd cleared the entire area of security staff.

'Hah, they're going to have to make some design changes to this place. I've overridden the security alarms, nice and easy. Not very secure as it turns out. This is exactly the distraction we need. Who is this guy?'

'This is my dad, Michael Brady. I can't believe he's here.'

He hugged his father again, as if to make sure he was real.

'Pleased to meet you, Michael.'

Richter held out his hand. Michael looked at him and paused. Then, cautiously, he held out his hand and squeezed Richter's hard.

'You rat us out and I'll kill you myself.'

He'd be no match for Richter, but the sentiment was understood.

'I'm the only way you're getting out of here, Michael. You need men like me in times like this. You don't get to pick and choose the things you have to do to stay alive. I've been in a war. I know how it goes.'

The shuttle emerged out of the tunnel and drew to a halt at the platform. On board were two Troopers who were immediately pulled off the train and disappeared into the frenzied crowd baying for their blood. The first group of prisoners piled into the shuttle and it set off for the centre of Fortrillium.

'We need to get back on the next one before they realize what's going on and send in the big guns,' said Richter. 'We'll get trapped in here if we're not careful.'

He started to move towards the edge of the platform, but never got there. There was the sound of a gunshot. Richter cried out and fell to the ground.

A bedraggled woman stepped out from the crowd, a gun in her hand and hatred in her eyes. She'd taken the weapon from one of the dead guards.

Alex and Michael stood back from Richter as he writhed on the floor, a pool of blood forming by his leg.

'You monster!' the woman screamed, stamping on his wounded leg. 'You thought you could get away with it. Well, you can't!'

She was out of control in her anger. Alex moved to try to calm her. She raised the gun and waved it at him.

'Can't we talk about this?' Michael urged, watching how

the gun kept moving back to Richter's head. 'We need this man alive if we're going to get out of here. You can come with us. What's your name?'

'Ask him if he knows who I am. I bet he doesn't. We're all meaningless to him.' She looked at Richter and hissed, 'Listen to my name now, because it's going to be the last thing you hear. I'm Laney Price. And you and my snake of a husband killed my babies.'

CHAPTER TEN

'Woah, you need to calm down!'

Richter held up his hands. He recognized her now. Her hair was dirty and unkempt, her clothes filthy and torn. But he'd seen that face before. Only this time she'd got a gun in her hand and the tables were turned.

Laney Price had dreamed of this moment. She could still see the smirk on Richter's face when he'd come into her house. There was only one man she wanted to kill more than Richter and that was her cockroach of a husband.

Alex stepped in to try to take some heat out of the situation. They still had to find Audra and rendezvous with Susan. They couldn't afford this delay.

'We have to get out,' he urged her. 'Richter is our best chance of escape, and—'

Laney shot her weapon into the air. She seemed surprised at its kick.

'Shut up!' she shouted. 'I don't want to hurt you and your friend, but this man – this scum – he gets what's coming to him.'

There were shots behind them – sustained gunfire and

everywhere panic and screaming. Three Troopers had stepped off the next shuttle to arrive and were firing at random into the crowd of prisoners waiting to board.

Richter tried to reason with Laney, his hand resting on his wounded leg.

'We have to get out of here, the place will soon be swarming with Troopers. Without me, you've got no chance of escaping.'

Laney looked at him, then to Alex and Michael, unsure what to do next. It was Evan she wanted most. She needed to find out why he'd betrayed them. He'd been there outside their apartment, watching, as they'd fired the stun gun at her. And she'd thought it was the old woman who'd snitched on them.

Alex had been watching the Troopers as they fired at the crowd. He suddenly shouted, 'That's Harley! The one without the helmet!'

There was more automatic gunfire, and a line of prisoners fell to the ground, dead or wounded. Harley's face showed the exaltation that he felt. The power, the control, the ability to take or spare life was like a drug to him.

The crowd was scattering, some taking refuge in the cages from which they'd escaped, others hiding in the office area. Harley scanned the platform, spotting Alex ahead of him, and next to him his father. He smiled. It couldn't be better, his position at Fortrillium would be secured. This new world was a place where he could flourish. Harley strode towards them, flanked by the other two Troopers. He saw Richter lying on the ground and recognized him immediately.

He levelled his gun at Laney. She saw him, but was slow to react. Richter saw he was about to shoot. With a superhuman effort he raised himself up and hurled himself at her, his massive bulk leaving her winded on the cold, concrete floor. He had no particular desire to save Laney's life, but by using this distraction, he could take her gun and move the situation in his favour. He rolled away, firing two shots one after the other. Both Troopers fell to the ground. He whipped round and pointed the weapon at Harley's head.

'Drop the gun!'

He watched as Harley's finger hovered on the trigger.

'You move to squeeze that trigger and you'll have a bullet right between your eyes.'

Harley looked at Richter and then at Alex and Michael. He didn't understand what was going on.

'I'm from Fortrillium! I'm like you, Mr Richter. I've come to rescue you and take Alex and his father to City Hall.'

'Put the gun down and shut up!'

Harley placed his weapon on the ground and raised his hands in the air. Laney was now struggling to her feet. Richter indicated that Alex and Michael should pick up their weapons and cover Harley. He held out his hand to help Laney up, grimacing as he did so. Alex saw that a patch of blood had seeped through the armored plates on his leather trousers.

'You're wounded!'

'It's only a graze. I'll be fine. But, Miss, you need to stop trying to kill me and muck in a bit. There are more of these guys coming. We have to get away from here.'

Laney nodded reluctantly. She saw that it was time to back down.

'So, Harley, why were you coming for Alex's father?' Richter asked.

Harley was silent.

Richter shot at his foot. A small piece of leather flew across the floor. Harley yelped and jumped back.

'I hit your boot, not your foot. Next time I take a toe. I need an answer. What do you want with Michael?'

'We were going to take him to City Hall ...' Harley began. 'Morgan wants him there.'

'Well, the good news is, Morgan is getting what he wants. Miss ... Laney did you say your name was? Get one of those Trooper uniforms on and grab their weapons. Harley, put on a helmet. I want your face covered. You keep your mouth shut and do exactly as you're told. One wrong move and I'll put a bullet in your spine. You'll be a cripple for the rest of your life. You'll wish you were dead. Understood?'

Harley looked at him. He knew this man meant what he said.

'Understood?' Richter asked again. 'Say it.'

'Understood,' Harley replied, his voice shaking. 'Please don't hurt me.'

The rest of the Troopers were filing onto the platform. They looked at Richter expectantly. Everybody knew who he was. Nobody was going to challenge him. He spoke to the Trooper in charge.

'We've secured the main area, but there are still hundreds of inmates unaccounted for. You need to take over and track them down. We have orders from Morgan to deliver this prisoner to City Hall.'

'Yes, sir,' the man responded without hesitation.

The small group headed towards the shuttle, Alex and Laney dressed as Troopers, Harley in front of them and Michael at the head of the pack, his hands loosely bound. He looked every bit the escorted prisoner. They walked unhindered towards the train, the sounds of gunshots disappearing behind them as the newly arrived security force set to work to restore order in The Soak.

It took only a few minutes to reach Fortrillium. As the shuttle pulled alongside the platform they looked out of the window to see piles of dead bodies, men and women, all gunned down before they could flee through the corridors. These were the prisoners who had left on the earlier shuttle. Alex was relieved he and his friends were with Richter. Richter knew what he was doing. Without him they would meet a similar brutal fate.

Dragging his injured leg behind him, Richter moved surprisingly rapidly through the corridors towards the hangar where the helicopters would be lined up ready for flight. He thought about Morgan. He needed to maintain the deception – the man would have no idea that he had turned. He pulled out his Comms device and started to type a message to his former colleague.

The cells have been secured. On our way to City Hall in a chopper. Have with me prisoner Brady and your man Harley.

He pressed Send.

At last they arrived in the cavernous hangar. Alex looked around him, frantically scanning the area for Carlos and Deena. They should be here by now. Where were they?

'We're leaving now!' Richter shouted. 'If your friends aren't here in the next five minutes, they're on their own. Come on, we're taking this one.'

He pointed at a helicopter with machine guns mounted on both sides. Underneath were missile launchers right and left. As if this wasn't enough, heavy duty guns were set on the small wings that protruded from the craft. Above them the roof of the hangar was wide open, flooding the space with daylight.

There was a pile of bulky black backpacks stacked near the chopper.

'Take what you can carry and get on board,' Richter commanded.

Gingerly he lifted himself into the pilot's seat, taking care not to knock his damaged leg as he did so. Alex gasped as he saw a series of crimson splashes on the ground where the injured man had been walking across the hangar. Laney had noticed too.

'He's badly hurt. I don't know how long he can keep going.' She paused and then said in a quiet voice, 'That was my doing. What was I thinking of? I didn't even have a plan when I shot at him. I was just so angry.'

Richter switched on the engine and the rotor blades started to turn.

Alex didn't answer Laney. He was examining the backpacks closely. He'd seen similar items on TV.

'These must be jet packs. Here, look. They have hand controls tucked in the sides. I hope he doesn't expect us to use them.'

'He's ready to fly that thing out of here,' said Michael. 'Your pals will be trapped inside Fortrillium if they don't come now.'

They could hear shots. Someone had entered the hangar and was firing a gun. Then shouting.

'Alex, it's us!'

Carlos's voice could barely be heard over the sound of the blades, which were now spinning fast. Alex waved both arms at Richter, desperate to catch his attention. He'd seen what was happening and gave Alex a thumbs up. The machine had already started to hover a few inches off the ground.

'There they are!' Alex yelled. 'And they've got Professor Haworth with them too. Quick. They're being chased. We've got to get them in the chopper. We've got to get away.'

Flashes of gunfire could be seen in the distance. Not far behind were Troopers, lots of them. Every second the gap was closing. Jasmine and Magnus were following Carlos as he dodged round the vehicles and storage containers in the hangar.

They were only twenty metres away.

'Quick, everyone into the helicopter!' Alex shouted over the sound of the machine.

Michael ran over first, opening up the door. He made sure Laney was safely on board. As Jasmine arrived, panting for breath, he reached down and pulled her up. Magnus clambered in after her.

Now reunited, Carlos and Alex stood side by side firing at the advancing Troopers. They would fight until the very last minute, trying to keep them at bay so the chopper could take off safely.

'What about Audra, Carlos? Any sign of Audra?' Alex asked his friend as he fired into the distance.

'She's gone, Alex,' Carlos said. 'We think they've taken her to City Hall.'

Alex was desperately disappointed, but there was no time to ask more questions. His dad was shouting at him to hurry. He had to get into the chopper.

Out of the corner of his eye, Carlos saw a Trooper raise his gun, pointing it directly at Alex's head. He leaped forward to push his friend out of the way and the bullet hit him instead. He screamed as blood spurted out of a wound in his leg.

Alex looked at Carlos as he lay on the ground.

'Carlos! Damn it!'

'Run, Alex!'

A second shot struck him in the shoulder.

'No!' Alex cried, stooping over his injured friend. 'I'm not leaving you. I'll never leave you.' He grabbed his other arm, trying to pull him up.

'Alex, we have to go!'

Michael was yelling at his son. He could see the main group of Troopers were almost upon them.

'No. I'm not leaving Carlos,' Alex shouted back.

Tears were streaming down his face. Carlos looked up at him.

'I love you, man. Now do you believe that the world's going to the devil? Do me a favour and finish this.'

Before Alex could reply, there was the crack of a gunshot and Carlos fell back, a Trooper's bullet through his head.

There was no time to register his shock and grief. Alex stumbled towards the chopper and his father's outstretched hand. He allowed himself to be hauled to safety.

As the machine lifted up and out of the open roof, Alex watched the dead body of his best friend becoming smaller and smaller. He swore to himself that he would have his vengeance on Fortrillium.

The chopper soared up above the skyscrapers. Through his tears, Alex looked down on Fortrillium. The structure was vast, and once they'd completed their takeover of City

Park it would have total domination of the cityscape. Why had he been so slow to understand what was going on? Carlos, Deena ... they'd both told him. But he'd ignored them, even when Audra disappeared, convincing himself that what was happening wasn't as sinister as they were suggesting.

He saw it clearly now. With Carlos dead and the horrors that he'd seen inside Fortrillium, there could be no happy ending. He couldn't keep his head down and hope it wouldn't happen. It was too late. Things had gone too far. It was time to face reality.

Burning with fury at Carlos's death, Alex wiped his eyes on his sleeve. Now was the time for action. He turned round to look at the others.

'Once we've met up with Deena and got Mum and Audra, then we head for Sector 15. Right away. We can't stay here a day longer.'

He looked at Jasmine.

'Professor Haworth, can you tell me what's happened to Audra? I need to know she's safe.'

'She's been through a lot, Alex. But, yes, she's still alive and I hope and pray she'll recover from the treatment she's endured.'

'Treatment? What treatment?'

'Prepare yourself for a shock, Alex. A man called Julius Labatt was conducting experiments on Audra. She was an extremely valuable test subject. She carries natural immunity to the virus. Audra could be the key to the survival of our species. Can you understand how important that makes her?'

'Where is she now?' interrupted Magnus.

'She was taken away by the Troopers,' Jasmine said. 'I think they were taking her to City Hall.'

'If I got my hands on that Labatt ...' said Alex, his voice shaking with anger.

'I know it won't give you much consolation, Alex,' Jasmine replied. 'But Carlos and I arranged for Labatt to have a taste of his own medicine. What he was doing to Audra in those labs amounted to torture. He went way beyond what was necessary from a scientific point of view.'

'I know Labatt,' Michael said. 'I've been on the receiving end of his experiments. The man is an animal. What have you done to him? Is he dead?'

'He soon will be,' Jasmine replied. 'We left him attached to a machine he had devised to deliver electric shocks of increasing severity. One of the tests he was running on Audra was to see how much pain she could withstand. He did it for his own sick pleasure, no other reason. Well, he's getting to try it out for himself now.'

'This is all my fault,' Magnus said. He'd looked troubled from the moment they'd reached the helicopter.

He turned to Jasmine.

'You shouldn't have done that to Labatt. It's making us as bad as they are. We have to stop what's happening. We can't allow this cycle of violence to continue. It has to end somewhere.'

Richter was looking over his shoulder, trying to get their attention.

'I'm going to drop you on the helipad on the roof of City Hall,' he shouted. 'I'll give you twenty minutes and then be back to pick you up. I'm going to a place I know by the river where I can fuel up. We'll need it to get to the border.'

He glanced at Alex and spoke more softly.

'I'm sorry about your friend, but you've got to grieve for him later. Now is not the time. Focus on getting your girl and finding your mother.'

Alex nodded. He stared out of the window, blinking back his tears. The city below them was beautiful. For a moment it was possible to believe none of this had happened, that it had all been a bad dream.

Richter was lowering the chopper. They could see the helipad beneath them. They put on their helmets and picked up their weapons. This was it. It was time to carry out the plan they had hatched only a few hours before. Alex checked the Comms device on his body armor. Twenty minutes. They'd have to be fast.

The helicopter touched down. They jumped out onto the roof and Richter lifted off again. On the roof were two Troopers. They seemed taken aback by their arrival. Michael saw them radioing for guidance, but it was a call they never completed. He pointed his gun: two shots and the roof was secured.

Now Richter had gone there was no natural leader. Alex took the initiative. Activity was the best way for him to block out images of Carlos's violent death.

'Magnus and Professor Haworth, you'll stand out without uniforms. You need to stay here and keep the helipad clear.'

'No problem!' Magnus said. 'We'll get these jet packs ready.'

'Dad, you and I will walk with Harley between us. Harley, you know what will happen if you step out of line.'

'Okay, but what is this plan?' Michael asked.

'We find Mum. We get Deena and we rescue Audra. Then we get back up here in twenty minutes.'

Even as he said it, Alex knew how ridiculous he sounded. He was speaking like a soldier, but he was just some kid from college. It was absurd. Crazy or not, it had to be done.

'Ready everyone. Eighteen minutes left now. Let's go!'

Alex hadn't thought far enough ahead to consider what would happen to Harley. He recognized that he was currency; he could fast-track them to the front of a queue.

There were Troopers everywhere. Alex hadn't realized how many there would be. As they reached the ground floor they could hear the President's voice booming through loud-speakers. Otherwise there were no other sounds, except for the occasional crackle of a Trooper's radio.

Alex looked at Harley.

'Make sure you behave. We'll let you go, but only when we have everybody safely in the chopper. I don't like you, but I don't wish you any harm.'

Harley mumbled assent. He was looking around, searching for a way out. He cursed his helmet. Without it he'd be able to signal to one of the security guards with his eyes.

I know that times have been difficult. I know that you have had to place your trust in me. And today, at long last, I can give you the news that you have been waiting for ...

The President's voice was assured and measured. He knew he had big news to deliver and he was making the most of it.

'I want you to go up to that Trooper over there and ask him where Morgan wants Dad. If you do anything to give the game away, I swear I'll ...'

Alex didn't know what he'd do. He didn't want Harley to force him into making a decision. He was relying on him to be too scared to give the game away.

Laney was looking around, taking in her surroundings.

Alex tapped her arm, urging her to focus. He averted his eyes from Harley, only for a few moments. But it was enough.

We are in the grip of a deadly plague. This plague was spread among us by an alien contact. Incredible though it seems, when we made contact with this alien race, we believed it would bring only good to this planet. But they brought with them a disease that is deadly to human beings. It mutates and becomes progressively more deadly. It has the capacity to wipe out all life on this planet ...

Suddenly Alex glimpsed movement, a disturbance in the hushed auditorium. Deena. It was Deena and Scorsese being marched out of the room and into the entrance hall. He gasped. This was his chance to rescue his friend. But Harley was ahead of him.

The good news is we have a solution, and that's what I am delighted to announce to you today. There is a single young woman who had helped us achieve this breakthrough, a breakthrough which will be made available to the citizens of Sector 4 first of all. Her name is Audra Woods and she is about to join me on this very stage. Audra Woods is the world's first known Immune and with her help we believe that we can create a vaccine that will help every citizen in this beloved State of ours—

Two gunshots rang out, amplified by the President's microphone. Henderson slumped lifeless to the floor. Seconds later, Alex watched Harley grasp the arm of the Trooper that he'd been speaking to, spin him round for cover and aim the weapon that was slung on the man's shoulder. He opened a spray of bullets, aiming for Alex, Laney and Michael.

Everywhere was panic, people screaming as they rushed for the exit, fighting each other to get out of the building. The President had been shot, in front of every-body, on the stage.

The cameras that had been relaying the event on the screens in the auditorium, and on the TV channels beyond City Hall, were suddenly trained on a huddle of Troopers. It seemed they had apprehended the assassin already. The horrified viewers watched in grim fascination as the lens focused on the face of the gunman. Only it wasn't a man, it was a woman. On the screens before them was the face of Susan Brady, the new head of Fortrillium security.

Meanwhile, out of sight of the cameras, one of Kincade's men was being swept out of the auditorium, an escort of Troopers smoothing his way to a swift exit. In his hand was a recently fired gun.

Alex, Michael and Laney pushed their way through the surging crowds to the entrance hall. Harley was chasing them, firing at random. They weaved from side to side to avoid his bullets.

Another shot rang out. Someone had fired a gun a few feet away from them. They saw Harley slump to his knees, a hole through the front of his helmet.

As they stared at him, frozen in shock at what they had just witnessed, a new voice boomed out from the loud-speakers.

This is Bryce Kincade. There is no need to panic. The danger is over. Please return to your seats. We have apprehended the gunman who has shot our beloved President. Order will be restored. I repeat, there is no need to panic. The danger is over.

'Alex! You've got to get out of here!'

It was a Trooper, a female. Alex recognized her voice.

'Simone?'

She was crying.

'I had to do it ... Harley ... he had it coming to him. Now find Deena and your mum and get away!'

'Thank you, Simone ...'

She was gone, lost in the confusion.

They had one big advantage, their cover wasn't blown. Half a dozen Troopers were huddled round Harley's body, trying to work out what had happened. They had no idea what to do next. They were the men who had been escorting Deena and Scorsese out of the auditorium. Alex couldn't believe his luck. Right in the middle of the chaos and panic he'd found himself next to two of the very people he had come to rescue.

He seized his opportunity.

'We'll take these prisoners,' he said confidently. He gestured towards Michael. 'We have this other man in custody already.'

The Troopers guarding Deena and Scorsese seemed relieved to relinquish responsibility for their charges. They felt vulnerable in the mayhem. Their priority was to save their own skins.

As soon as the Troopers moved away, Alex spoke.

'Deena, it's me, Alex. Stay calm. We're getting you out of here. Where's Mum?'

'Alex, thank God, I thought Evan had messed every-thing up for us—'

'That wouldn't be Evan Price, would it?' Laney interrupted.

'Yes, why?'

'Where is he? I have a message to deliver to him.'

'In the auditorium, I think. Be careful, he's dangerous.'

'Not half as dangerous as I am.'

Laney turned her back on the group and started to run

through the crowd back into the auditorium. Alex let her go. There was no time to waste.

He held Deena's shoulders and looked into her eyes. He needed to be sure she'd follow his instructions.

'Deena, go with my dad, head up the stairs to the helipad on the roof. Be as quick as you can. I'll meet you there.'

'What about you, Mr Scorsese?' Deena asked.

'I won't be going with you, Deena. I'm staying. We need a new President now, and I have to be part of that process. If people like me don't stay, Fortrillium will have won and everything we stand for, human rights, democracy, will have been defeated. I can't let that happen.'

Michael took Deena's hand and led her to the staircase.

'Make sure you bring Audra back,' Deena called over her shoulder. She wanted to stay and fight to free her friend.

'Go, Deena!' Alex said, sensing her doubt. 'I have my body armor for cover, and they'd spot you a mile off. Go with Dad. Trust me.'

He watched them start to climb the stairs and then looked at the clock on his Comms device. There were four minutes remaining.

Scorsese had gone into the auditorium ahead of him. It was now less than half full. A few members of the public had stayed, encouraged to remain by Kincade's words. The majority of the people left were politicians, cordoned off in their own area, anxious to leave but held in their seats by Troopers. Kincade was on the stage, President Henderson's dead body at his feet, James Morgan at his side.

Behind them, drugged, dazed, completely unaware of what was going on, stood Audra. They'd cleaned her up and dressed her carefully so that her wounds didn't show.

Councillors, thank you for remaining.

Kincade was addressing the politicians in the seats below him. He was in his natural environment on the stage, commanding the attention of those who were left and at the same time playing to the cameras, which continued to broadcast the events as they unfolded. His voice filled the auditorium.

Under the amended Constitution of Sector 4, after the tragic demise of President Lance Henderson, it befalls me to oversee the swearing-in of our new interim President. My proposal is for James Morgan to step into place as a temporary measure. In times of crisis, such as today, we may agree his appointment where we are quorate – as we are right now. So my proposal is to swear in James Morgan as acting President of Sector 4, pending other arrangements in more settled times. Those in favour?

Kincade's gaze swept over the assembled politicians. They looked at each other, uncertain of what to do. Some held their hands up straightaway, knowing how this would play out. Others waited, hoping for a cue of some kind. The surrounding Troopers readied their weapons.

Alex paused to listen and, as he did so, he saw two Troopers hustling a woman away from the room. As she turned her head, he saw it was his mother. He had to reach her. He started to move towards her, creeping behind the rows of chairs, desperate to avoid being spotted.

'That's enough!' came a voice from the back of the auditorium. It was Scorsese. Looking straight ahead, he strode down the central aisle towards the stage. The man was a troublemaker. Kincade exchanged glances with Morgan. How would they deal with this man?

Suddenly a shout broke the silence.

'She's got a gun!'

A single shot rang out, followed by a burst of automatic

machine-gun fire. Susan had broken free of her captors. She'd taken a weapon and killed both of them. Alex called to her.

'Mum! It's me, Alex!'

Susan turned and rushed towards her son.

'Thank God! Alex, you're here!'

'We have to go, Mum. Quick, to the roof. We've only got a minute left.'

It was all happening too fast. As he raced out of the auditorium, dragging his mother by the hand, Alex knew he couldn't abandon Audra. There was no time to search for her now. He would see his friends make their escape in the helicopter and then return to find Audra, his girl.

The entrance hall was eerily quiet. Harley's bloodied body lay where Simone had shot him.

'Up the stairs! Come on!' Alex said.

They were late. Richter had been perfectly clear about the timings. Alex ran anyway. Perhaps he would wait for a few minutes.

They had to climb four flights of stairs. By the time they finally reached the rooftop, they were both gasping for breath.

They stepped out onto the roof. It was quiet, no sign of Michael, Magnus, Deena or Jasmine Haworth. They were alone. In the distance they could hear the sound of helicopter blades. They were two minutes late. Richter had left without them.

Suddenly, out of nowhere, a chopper roared over the rooftop, closely followed by a second. They were flying low. Alex and Susan ducked.

'Richter is in the first helicopter – Dad's in there with him. They're being chased!'

'You found your father! How?'

'He was locked up in Fortrillium. They've built a prison in there. We got him out, and now he's in that helicopter.'

Susan and Alex looked into the distance. There were now three black objects in the sky. They were too far away to see which helicopter was which.

There was a sudden flash of light and then one of them spiraled downwards in a ball of fire.

Susan covered her face with her hands. She couldn't bear to watch.

'Please, not Dad!' Alex cried.

They waited. The two remaining black forms were getting closer. Was it the Fortrillium helicopters returning to base having neutralized the fugitives?

There was a movement behind them. Alex turned round. It was a Trooper, in the process of removing his helmet with one hand, while supporting his companion with the other. It was Audra and she could hardly stand up.

The helmet was off.

'Simone!'

The girl spoke rapidly. She didn't have time to hang around.

'She's sedated, Alex. She doesn't recognize me. But she's alive. I have to get out of here now, before they find me with you. Good luck, Alex. I'm sorry for everything.'

Simone disappeared down the stairwell as fast as she'd arrived.

Audra swayed, she looked like she was sleepwalking. Alex put his arm round her shoulders. The roar of the choppers was getting louder and louder. They had to shout to be heard above the noise.

'Mum, it's Richter! They've come back for us. Help me with Audra.'

The chopper hovered above the helipad. The cabin

door was thrown open and Michael was shouting at them to get in. The second helicopter buzzed over them, bursts of machine-gun fire shattering the slates on the surrounding rooftops.

Alex and Susan half carried Audra over to the chopper and Michael hauled her on board. His wife and son followed. Barely were their feet off the ground than the machine soared into the air, flying over the lawns of City Hall and towards the skyscrapers.

'We've got company!' Richter shouted.

Alex looked at him. He could see he was in a bad way. His face was grey, beads of sweat standing out on his fore-head. By his foot was a pool of blood.

'I'm flying to the border. Strap yourselves in, put on the headsets. It's going to be some ride.'

'Richter, I'm worried about you,' said Jasmine. 'You've lost too much blood, we need to get you some medical attention.'

'Not until we cross the border. Unless anybody else can fly this thing?'

There was silence. They needed him and they knew it.

Richter was keeping the chopper low, flying in and out of the skyscrapers, scanning the skies for their pursuer. There was another helicopter out there somewhere.

'I need to neutralize the nano-devices,' Magnus said. 'They can harm us if they're still active when we fly across the state border. Who's had the latest VaXX?'

Except for Alex and Deena, everyone had had it. Magnus took a handheld device from his bag. He activated it via his thumbprint and it buzzed into life, its shaft glowing with an icy blue light. He set to work. Thrown from side to side in the cabin, he struggled to hold the device steady, but once he had configured it, the nano-devices were neutralized as easily as they'd been placed inside them.

'The devices stay inside you, but they're harmless now,' he explained. 'Fortrillium can't track you and they can't hurt you either. You can get them extracted in Sector 15.'

The buildings were lower in height now. They were nearing the outskirts of the city.

'What about you?' Jasmine asked, taking Magnus's hand. There had been no time for a reunion. They'd barely spoken since he and Carlos had rescued her from the lab.

'I'm fine. I'll be fine—'

He suddenly stopped talking as the chopper lurched to the right, dodging a missile aiming straight for them. The weapon whistled past and exploded into the side of an office building ahead of them.

'Hold tight!' Richter shouted. 'There might be more where that came from. Magnus, you need to see what you can do with the girl. She'll need to be alert if we get into trouble.'

He was doing his best to sound bright and in control, but Jasmine knew the truth. Richter was fading.

'What have they done to her?' Alex asked. 'Is she drugged?'

'No, I don't think so,' Jasmine replied. 'What do you think, Magnus?'

'I think it's electronic ... one moment.'

He put his hand into his bag and brought out a set of pliers.

Magnus felt about at the base of Audra's neck then moved the pliers towards the top of her spine, pinched the ends together and held up a small device. There were two fine wires attached to a flickering metal disc. As he held it up, the flashing lights on it dulled and ceased.

'A neural implant,' he announced. 'She'll be back with us soon.'

The helicopter veered to the side again, this time to the left.

'We need to get out of Sector 4 airspace. They won't follow us over the border.'

His voice was weak now. He was struggling to stay conscious.

'Richter, are you alright? Are you going to make it?' Jasmine asked. Alex saw the worry on her face.

'Alex?'

Audra had spoken. It was the first time he'd heard her voice since the video.

'Audra!'

'Where are we? What's happened?'

Alex squeezed her hand. It was the first kindness she'd felt in almost a year.

'We're getting you away from Fortrillium. This will be soon be over.'

As he spoke, two jets appeared on either side of the helicopter and then suddenly veered upwards.

'Okay, life gets difficult now,' Richter said. 'These guys will be hard to outrun. Put those backpacks on, but be careful. Whatever you do, don't press the ignition buttons until you're outside.'

They looked at each other. Alex pulled out one of the packs that had been stowed to the side.

'You're kidding me?' he said.

'Put them on!' Richter repeated. 'I think you're going to need them in the next few minutes.'

'But there are only seven of them,' Deena shouted, searching around for a place where more might have been stored. 'And there are eight of us!'

'That's alright, I'm travelling in this thing,' Richter replied.

The chopper lurched to the right, throwing them against the door.

A stream of bullets struck the side of the chopper. The machine careered from side to side as a second missile flew by.

'Richter! They hit—'

'Get out!' Richter shouted. 'I can't hold this much longer. I'm going as high as I can. You're going to have to jump. Open the door, jump out and press the ignition button. Good luck!'

Richter brought the helicopter round in a circle and began to climb steeply upwards. They were well away from the city now, out in the open and above the sort of fields where the Matiz family had once been able to make their living.

Alex froze. He was terrified at the prospect of leaping out of the moving helicopter.

'Go! Now!' Richter yelled.

'Michael threw open the cabin door as Richter held the chopper as steady as he could. In the distance the roar of the jets could be heard. They were coming in for the kill. There was no way they were letting that helicopter cross over the border.

'Jump!' Richter shouted. 'Do it now or you die!'

Susan went first, Michael next, followed by a white-faced Deena. Magnus pushed Jasmine out of the door and followed directly behind her. Alex looked at Audra.

'I love you,' he said. 'I'm sorry it took so long to come for you.'

'I'm so glad you came, Alex. Whatever happens, I want you to know that I love you too.'

She jumped.

The helicopter that had been keeping up the chase alongside the jets suddenly reared up at their side and started to spray them with machine-gun fire. Richter slumped over the controls and the machine began to spiral downwards.

For a split second Alex hesitated. He had no time to process what he saw. He turned and jumped, immediately plummeting towards the ground below. He knew he had to press the ignition button, but the fall had taken his breath away. Next to him the helicopter hurtled downwards, exploding in a ball of flames as it hit the ground. Alex finally found the button and pressed it.

They gathered round to watch the footage. It had been smuggled over the border; it was a video that everybody wanted to see.

Sector 4 had closed its borders. Vast walls were going up. They'd become a silent state. Nobody knew what was going on any more.

'Okay, everybody. Let's take a look, shall we?'

The video was poor quality, but clear enough. It was news footage. President Lance Henderson was on stage, giving his speech. There was a shot from the crowd. Confusion. More shots. Whoever had filmed this had been in the public seating area inside the auditorium. For a couple of minutes there was just a blurred screen. More shouting, more shots. A view of Bryce Kincade on the stage. James Morgan joining him. Audra in the background, dazed, unaware of what was going on. Then, Scorsese's voice, challenging Kincade.

Suddenly, loud and clear, they heard the voice of the person doing the recording.

'How could you kill our babies, you monster!'

'That's Laney!' Michael cried.

The video blurred again and all that could be heard was Laney's voice, screaming abuse.

Then another shot. The one that started the second panic.

The video footage came to an abrupt end.

Another video came on the screen. This time it was much more polished, part of a newsreel. It was showing public hangings. They recognized the location. It was outside the gates to Fortrillium. They were hanging them by chains. Deena winced as she saw Scorsese's face on the screen, defiant to the end. As Simone's terrified image appeared next, she burst into tears. She too was hanged, along with a number of politicians who'd been branded as traitors.

This was the place they'd called their home. It was descending into barbarism. Innocent people were being killed.

They'd escaped with their lives. As one-by-one they'd leaped into the unknown, they'd pressed the ignition buttons as directed by Richter. As they pressed the buttons, the jet packs flared up and hand controls emerged to either side. A headset moved over their ears from above and a calm voice asked them to set their destination.

'Sector 15!' they'd all shouted. That was where they'd agreed to meet.

That was all they had to do. The jet packs took their weight, set the route and lowered their level to an altitude that took them just above house height.

They watched Richter's helicopter explode in a ball of

flames as it crashed to the ground. They were hovering too low for the jets to pursue them and they'd crossed the border by the time any other defensive action could be launched. It wasn't until they landed that they realized Alex wasn't with them. No one had seen what had happened to him.

A month passed. Audra was given urgent medical attention and, only when she was fit enough, Jasmine and her team began to conduct experiments. Having an Immune in their care could give them the breakthrough they needed.

Michael shaved his beard and cut his hair. Gradually he regained his strength. Soon he began to look like the man that Susan remembered and they started to rebuild their relationship bit by bit. But they'd lost Alex. They'd lost their only surviving son.

Then, one day, the news they dared not hope for. Alex had been found, walking across fields not far from where Sector 15 joined Sector 4. His jet pack had been damaged in the blast, but it had got him over the border where he reported seeing the beginnings of huge walls going up. Alex was safe. He was hungry, filthy, exhausted – but alive.

They watched as the video came to an end. As the walls surrounding Sector 4 were getting higher, so the resistance was growing. People were risking their lives – good people like Carlos, Scorsese and Laney – they were standing up against the bullies. However long it took, whatever it took, so long as there were people who were prepared to fight back, they'd make it. Humanity would survive.

Alex needed time alone. He felt sick as he watched the hangings on the screen. If it hadn't been for Laney that would probably be him and his mother too. What had happened to Laney? They had to assume that she was dead, and that it was her husband that she had shot in City Hall. At least she'd gone to her grave avenging her children.

Evan, it seemed, was an opportunist. Another Harley, seeking to improve his own fortunes in times of crisis – even if it meant sacrificing his own family. Deena reckoned he must have been working as an informer, but she'd never have guessed it. He played the role of treacherous rat with ease.

Jasmine Haworth had thrown herself into her research work, finally reunited with her husband, who dedicated himself immediately to the resistance efforts.

Alex looked at the family photo that his mum had rescued from the apartment before she'd fled. It was on the table of their new quarters now, a constant reminder of what they'd left behind. As the world crumbled around them in the months that followed, he would continue to look at it. It was a sign of hope when everything else seemed to be falling down around them.

He shook his head and sighed as he thought of everyone he'd lost: Carlos, Simone, Scorsese, Richter – even Harley. So much death, so much suffering.

They'd done what they could. They'd rescued Audra, the world's first known Immune, from the evil, repressive regime that was Fortrillium. She was now with scientists who would share with others what they learned from her. She was humanity's best hope. Together they could bring the planet back from the brink of disaster that was Phase 6.

Discover what happened before Phase 6 in The Secret Bunker Trilogy …

Who is Magnus and what was he involved in before the

plague struck? Learn about the events leading up to Phase 6 in this action-packed apocalyptic trilogy.

Find out about the post-plague world in The Grid Trilogy …
James Morgan's lust for power is far from over and the plague will wreak a devastating toll across the planet. Will anybody survive and what sort of monster will Fortrillium become? Discover more secrets in this fast-paced, sci-fi trilogy.

AUTHOR NOTES

Phase 6 is my most recent science fiction book and after writing several thrillers it took a little while to get back into the flow.

However, I was really keen to write a sci-fi novel which bridged the worlds of The Secret Bunker and The Grid.

Phase 6 is set after the events in The Secret Bunker and before the apocalyptic scenes in The Grid.

I wanted to show the world turning sour, but the source of this threat to the earth is something different than in The Secret Bunker, though it does actually stem from events in that book.

There are two characters who appear in both trilogies.

One is Magnus who is a central character in The Secret Bunker Trilogy, the other is James Morgan who goes on to have a much bigger role in The Grid Trilogy, but here we see him as a junior, just beginning to gain his considerable power.

I always loved the character of Magnus in The Secret Bunker Trilogy and so I was keen to include him in a story again.

In The Secret Bunker I wanted to show him as a man who was capable of much but who had signed deals and made arrangements in his past which didn't sit well with his conscience.

In Phase 6 he's very much back on form, an influential figure and one who is making amazing technical break-throughs.

In The Secret Bunker Trilogy the threat to the world is an environmental one and to a certain extent one that comes off-planet.

But having resolved those issues in The Secret Bunker Trilogy what could possibly come back to bite the earth and create the disruption that we see Phase 6?

Well, as it turns out, it's a plague and one that capable of wiping out the whole planet.

The reason I like to flit between thrillers and science fiction is because in my sci-fi I can extrapolate observations and ideas that I have about everyday life and insert them into fictional situations.

So for instance in Phase 6 I was able to reflect my thoughts about Amazon's Alexa product which I have observed in a number of my friends' and families' houses.

Now, I love to be an early adopter with all things technical but Alexa - and the Apple and Google equivalents - are where I draw my personal line in the sand.

With the way that politics have become divisive in recent years it doesn't take much of a leap of imagination to consider how these devices might be used for listening, perhaps to weed out political opponents or people who hold different views from those in power.

In the scene where Deena visits Scorsese in his apart-ment, she immediately spots Scorsese's Model 13 device.

Now, this is slightly more advanced than Amazon's

Alexa model, but the Model 13 is kitted out with the voice audio files of Scorsese's deceased wife.

Deena comments on how personalising the devices with the voices of loved ones makes them seem less sinister but in actual fact they are listening devices being used by forces planning to control their lives.

I did the same thing with the VAXX program, I didn't want to get deeply embroiled with pro-vaccination and anti-vaccination arguments, I simply wanted to make the point that if you wanted to fit your citizens with tracking devices an excellent way of doing that would be to create a health scare and then strongly promote a program of immunisation.

Now, in Phase 6 the threat to human life is real, however it hasn't stopped the powers that be hijacking the latest injections with tracking devices.

In my first draft of this book I made the location New York, but I needed to revert back to a generic location because in true science fiction fashion, I was keen to make this book an everyman story and one that could be taking place in any metropolitan city throughout the world.

Every major city (more or less) has a large river running through it and a huge park somewhere its centre, so when I wrote the story I was thinking about Central Park and the skyscrapers which surround it, however it could be anywhere else in the world that fits this description.

I also wanted to imagine a world falling to pieces bit by bit and consider what might happen firstly in terms of what disruptions the citizens would notice and secondly, how it would impact on their lives.

So mobile phones are sketchy, food is becoming short in supply and because of that the city is looking at commandeering farming and food sources so that they can control these factors as things get worse.

I'm fascinated by how things would fall apart in a real scenario like this - for instance if bird flu or swine flu were to take a grip of the world.

I have a feeling that we would have a greater sense of a military presence pretty soon and things would get stricter and harsher in no time at all.

I also suspect that protests and dissenting voices might be criticised, in order to encourage everybody else to fall in line, and I do try to reflect this in the story.

Science fiction is a great way for writers to take things in our everyday lives and let their imagination run riot, considering where they might end up in a dystopian scenario.

Essentially though, Phase 6 was written to be non-stop, action-packed thrill of a ride.

I wanted to pack it with likeable characters, people whose motives are ambiguous, strong female leads and people who are just plain bad.

I like to explore relationships in my books, between siblings, partners, authority and friends and I do like to put my protagonists under extreme pressure and force them to confront truths and grow personally as a consequence of what happens in each story.

If you enjoyed reading Phase 6 and you'd like to stay touch, please register for my email updates at https://paul-teague.net/scifi.

In the meantime, thank you for reading Phase 6 and I hope that you will check out one of my other books soon.

Paul Teague

ABOUT THE AUTHOR

Hi, I'm Paul Teague, the author of The Secret Bunker Trilogy and The Grid Trilogy as well as several other stand-alone psychological thrillers such as Burden of Guilt, Dead of Night and One Fatal Error.

I'm a former broadcaster and journalist with the BBC, but I have also worked as a primary school teacher, a disc jockey, a shopkeeper, a waiter and a sales rep.

I've loved sci-fi all of my life, starting with the Danny Dunn books and progressing to the huge franchises such as Terminator, Star Trek, Babylon 5, The Hunger Games and The Maze Runner series.

Be first to hear about new books and special offers:
https://paulteague.net